SAD CYPRESS

Agatha Christie was born in Torquay of an English mother and an American father. Her first novel was *The Mysterious Affair at Styles*, written towards the end of the First World War, in which she served as a V.A.D. in France. It was in this book that she created the brilliant little Belgian detective with the egg shaped head and the impressive moustaches, Hercule Poirot, who was destined to become the most popular detective in crime fiction since Sherlock Holmes.

In 1926 she wrote what is still considered her masterpiece, *The Murder of Roger Ackroyd*. This was the first of her books to be published by William Collins, who have been her publishers ever since. Her 73rd detective novel, *Elephants Can Remember*, appeared in November 1972.

Agatha Christie, now in her eighties, is married to Sir Max Mallowan, a well-known archaeologist, and apart from her writing, her husband's subject, archaeology, remains her chief outside interest. They live in a beautiful house in Devon, overlooking the river Dart, and they also have a home in London.

AGATHA CHRISTIE

Sad Cypress

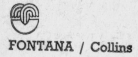

FONTANA / Collins

First published 1933
First issued in Fontana Books 1959
Thirteenth Impression August 1973

© 1939, 1940 Agatha Christie Mallowan

Printed in Great Britain
Collins Clear-Type Press London and Glasgow

To Peter *and* Peggy McLeod

Come away, come away, death,
   And in sad cypress let me be laid;
Fly away, fly away, breath;
   I am slain by a fair cruel maid.
My shroud of white, stuck all with yew
     O prepare it;
My part of death no one so true;
     Did share it.

SHAKESPEARE

PROLOGUE

'Elinor Katharine Carlisle. You stand charged upon this in-dictment with the murder of Mary Gerrard upon the 27th of July last. Are you guilty or not guilty?'

Elinor Carlisle stood very straight, her head raised. It was a graceful head, the modelling of the bones sharp and well defined. The eyes were a deep vivid blue, the hair black. The brows had been plucked to a faint thin line.

There was a silence—quite a noticeable silence.

Sir Edwin Bulmer, Counsel for the Defence, felt a thrill of dismay.

He thought:

'My God, she's going to plead guilty. . . . She's lost her nerve. . . .'

Elinor Carlisle's lips parted. She said:

'Not guilty.'

Counsel for the Defence sank back. He passed a hand-kerchief over his brow, realising that it had been a near shave.

Sir Samuel Attenbury was on his feet, outlining the case for the Crown.

'May it please your lordship, gentlemen of the jury, on the 27th of July, at half-past three in the afternoon, Mary Ger-rard died at Hunterbury, Maidensford . . .'

His voice ran on, sonorous and pleasing to the ear. It lulled Elinor almost into unconsciousness. From the simple and con-cise narrative, only an occasional phrase seeped through to her conscious mind.

'. . . Case a peculiarly simple and straightforward one . . .

'. . . It is the duty of the Crown . . . prove motive and oppor-tunity. . . .

'. . . No one, as far as can be seen, had any motive to kill this unfortunate girl, Mary Gerrard, except the accused. A young girl of a charming disposition—liked by everybody—without, one would have said, an enemy in the world. . . .'

Mary, Mary Gerrard! How far away it all seemed now. Not real any longer. . . .

'. . . Your attention will be particularly directed to the fol-lowing considerations:

1. What opportunities and means had the accused for ad-

ministering poison?

2. What motive had she for so doing?

'It will be my duty to call before you witnesses who can help you to form a true conclusion on these matters. . . .

'. . . As regards the poisoning of Mary Gerrard, I shall endeavour to show you that *no one had any opportunity* to commit this crime except the accused. . . .'

Elinor felt as though imprisoned in a thick mist. Detached words came drifting through the fog.

'. . . Sandwiches . . .

'. . . Fish paste . . .

'. . . Empty house. . . .'

The words stabbed through the thick enveloping blanket of Elinor's thoughts—pin-pricks through a heavy muffling veil. . . .

The court. Faces. Rows and rows of faces! One particular face with a big black moustache and shrewd eyes. Hercule Poirot, his head a little on one side, his eyes thoughtful, was watching her.

She thought: He's trying to see just exactly *why* I did it. . . . He's trying to get inside my head to see what I thought—what I felt. . . .

Felt . . .? A little blur—a slight sick sense of shock. . . . Roddy's face—his dear, *dear* face with its long nose, its sensitive mouth . . . Roddy! Always Roddy—always, ever since she could remember . . . since those days at Hunterbury amongst the raspberries and up in the warren and down by the brook. Roddy—Roddy—Roddy. . . .

Other faces! Nurse O'Brien, her mouth slightly open, her freckled fresh face thrust forward. Nurse Hopkins looking smug—smug and implacable. Peter Lord's face—Peter Lord —so kind, so sensible, so—so *comforting*! But looking now— what was it—*lost*? Yes—lost! Minding—minding all this frightfully! While she herself, the star performer, didn't mind at all!

Here she was, quite calm and cold, standing in the dock, accused of murder. She was in court.

Something stirred; the folds of blanket round her brain lightened—became mere wraiths. In *court!* . . . *People*. . . .

People leaning forward, their lips parted a little, their eyes agog, staring at her, Elinor, with a horrible ghoulish enjoyment—listening with a kind of slow, cruel relish to what that tall man with the Jewish nose was saying about her.

'The facts in this case are extremely easy to follow and are not in dispute. I shall put them before you quite simply. From the very beginning . . .'

Elinor thought:

'The beginning. . . . The beginning? The day that horrible anonymous letter came! *That* was the beginning of it. . . .'

PART ONE

CHAPTER ONE

I

An anonymous letter!

Elinor Carlisle stood looking down at it as it lay open in her hand. She'd never had such a thing before. It gave one an unpleasant sensation. Ill-written, badly spelt, on cheap pink paper.

This is to Warn You (it ran),
I'm naming no Names but there's Someone sucking up to your Aunt and if you're not kareful you'll get Cut Out of Everything. Girls Are very Artful and Old Ladies is Soft when Young Ones suck up to Them and Flatter them What I say is You'd best come down and see for Yourself whats Going On its not right you and the Young Gentleman should be Done Out of What's yours—and She's Very Artful and the Old Lady might Pop off at any time.
Well-Wisher.

Elinor was still staring at this missive, her plucked brows drawn together in distaste, when the door opened. The maid announced, 'Mr. Welman,' and Roddy came in.

Roddy! As always when she saw Roddy, Elinor was conscious of a slightly giddy feeling, a throb of sudden pleasure, a feeling that it was incumbent upon her to be very matter-of-fact and unemotional. Because it was so very obvious that Roddy, although he loved her, didn't feel about her the way she felt about him. The first sight of him did something to her, twisted her heart round so that it almost hurt. Absurd that a man—an ordinary, yes, a perfectly ordinary young man—should be able to do that to one! That the mere look of him should set the world spinning, that his voice should make you want—just a little—to cry. . . . Love surely should be a pleasurable emotion—not something that hurt you by its intensity. . . .

One thing was clear: one must be very, very careful to be

off-hand and casual about it all. Men didn't like devotion and adoration. Certainly Roddy didn't.

She said lightly:

'Hallo, Roddy!'

Rody said:

'Hallo, darling. You're looking very tragic. Is it a bill?'

Elinor shook her head.

Roddy said:

'I thought it might be—midsummer, you know—when the fairies dance, and the accounts rendered come tripping along!'

Elinor said:

'It's rather horrid. It's an anonymous letter.'

Roddy's brows went up. His keen fastidious face stiffened and changed. He said—a sharp, disgusted exclamation:

'No!'

Elinor said again:

'It's rather horrid. . . .'

She moved a step towards her desk.

'I'd better tear it up, I suppose.'

She could have done that—she almost did—for Roddy and anonymous letters were two things that ought not to come together. She might have thrown it away and thought no more about it. He would not have stopped her. His fastidiousness was far more strongly developed than his curiosity.

But on an impulse Elinor decided differently. She said:

'Perhaps, though, you'd better read it first. Then we'll burn it. It's about Aunt Laura.'

Roddy's eyebrows rose in surprise.

'Aunt Laura?'

He took the letter, read it, gave a frown of distaste, and handed it back.

'Yes,' he said. 'Definitely to be burnt! How extraordinary people are!'

Elinor said:

'One of the servants, do you think?'

'I suppose so.' He hesitated. 'I wonder who—who the person is—the one they mention?'

Elinor said thoughtfully:

'It must be Mary Gerrard, I think.'

Roddy frowned in an effort of remembrance.

'Mary Gerrard? Who's she?'

'The daughter of the people at the lodge. You must remember her as a child? Aunt Laura was always fond of the girl,

12

and took an interest in her. She paid for her schooling and for various extras—piano lessons and French and things.'

Roddy said:

'Oh, yes, I remember her now: scrawny kid, all legs and arms, with a lot of messy fair hair.'

Elinor nodded.

'Yes, you probably haven't seen her since those summer holidays when Mum and Dad were abroad. You've not been down at Hunterbury as often as I have, of course, and she's been abroad *au pair* in Germany lately, but we used to rout her out and play with her when we were all kids.'

'What's she like now?' asked Roddy.

Elinor said:

'She's turned out very nice-looking. Good manners and all that. As a result of her education, you'd never take her for old Gerrard's daughter.'

'Gone all lady-like, has she?'

'Yes. I think, as a result of that, she doesn't get on very well at the lodge. Mrs. Gerrard died some years ago, you know, and Mary and her father don't get on. He jeers at her schooling and her "fine ways." '

Roddy said irritably:

'People never dream what harm they may do by "educating" someone! Often it's cruelty, not kindness!'

Elinor said:

'I suppose she *is* up at the house a good deal. . . . She reads aloud to Aunt Laura, I know, since she had her stroke.'

Roddy said:

'Why can't the nurse read to her?'

Elinor said with a smile:

'Nurse O'Brien's got a brogue you can cut with a knife! I don't wonder Aunt Laura prefers Mary.'

Roddy walked rapidly and nervously up and down the room for a minute or two. Then he said:

'You know, Elinor, I believe we ought to go down.'

Elinor said with a slight recoil:

'Because of this——?'

'No, no—not at all. Oh, damn it all, one must be honest, *yes*! Foul as that communication is, there *may* be some truth behind it. I mean, the old girl is pretty ill——'

'Yes, Roddy.'

He looked at her with his charming smile—admitting the fallibility of human nature. He said:

'And the money *does* matter—to you and me, Elinor.'

She admitted it quickly:

'Oh, it does.'

He said seriously:

'It's not that I'm mercenary. But, after all, Aunt Laura herself has said over and over again that you and I are her only family ties. You're her own niece, her brother's child, and I'm her husband's nephew. She's always given us to understand that at her death all she's got would come to one or other—or more probably both—of us. And—and it's a pretty large sum, Elinor.'

'Yes,' said Elinor thoughtfully. 'It must be.'

'It's no joke keeping up Hunterbury.' He paused. 'Uncle Henry was what you'd call, I suppose, comfortably off when he met your Aunt Laura. But she was an heiress. She and your father were both left very wealthy. Pity your father speculated and lost most of his.'

Elinor sighed.

'Poor Father never had much business sense. He got very worried over things before he died.'

'Yes, your Aunt Laura had a much better head than he had. She married Uncle Henry and they bought Hunterbury, and she told me the other day that she'd been exceedingly lucky always in her investments. Practically nothing had slumped.'

'Uncle Henry left all he had to her when he died, didn't he?'

Roddy nodded.

'Yes, tragic his dying so soon. And she's never married again. Faithful old bean. And she's always been very good to us. She's treated me as if I was her nephew by blood. If I've been in a hole she's helped me out; luckily I haven't done that *too* often!'

'She's been awfully generous to me, too,' said Elinor gratefully.

Roddy nodded.

'Aunt Laura,' he said, 'is a brick. But, you know, Elinor, perhaps without meaning to do so, you and I live pretty extravagantly, considering what our means really are!'

She said ruefully:

'I suppose we do. . . . Everything costs so much—clothes and one's face—and just silly things like cinemas and cocktails —and even gramophone records!'

Roddy said:

'Darling, you *are* one of the lilies of the field, aren't you?

14

You toil not, neither do you spin!'

Elinor said:

'Do you think I ought to, Roddy?'

He shook his head.

'I like you as you are: delicate and aloof and ironical. I'd hate you to go all earnest. I'm only saying that if it weren't for Aunt Laura you probably would be working at some grim job.'

He went on:

'The same with me. I've got a job, of sorts. Being with Lewis & Hume is not too arduous. It suits me. I preserve my self-respect by having a job; but—mark this—but I don't worry about the future because of my expectations—from Aunt Laura.'

Elinor said:

'We sound rather like human leeches!'

'Nonsense! We've been given to understand that some day we shall have money—that's all. Naturally, that fact influences our conduct.'

Elinor said thoughtfully:

'Aunt Laura has never told us definitely just *how* she has left her money?'

Roddy said:

'That doesn't matter! In all probability she's divided it between us; but if that isn't so—if she's left all of it or most of it to you as her own flesh and blood—why, then, darling, I shall share in it, because *I*'m going to marry you—and if the old pet thinks the majority should go to me as the male representative of the Welmans, that's still all right, because *you're* marrying *me*.'

He grinned at her affectionately. He said:

'Lucky we happen to love each other. You do love me, don't you, Elinor?'

'Yes.'

She said it coldly, almost primly.

'Yes!' Roddy mimicked her. 'You're adorable, Elinor. That little air of yours—aloof—untouchable—*la Princesse Lointaine*. It's that quality of yours that made me love you, I believe.'

Elinor caught her beath. She said, 'Is it?'

'Yes.' He frowned. 'Some women are so—oh, I don't know —so damned possessive—so—so dog-like and devoted—their emotions slopping all over the place! I'd hate that. With you

I never know—I'm never sure—any minute you might turn round in that cool, detached way of yours and say you'd changed your mind—quite coolly, like that—without batting an eyelash! You're a fascinating creature, Elinor. You're like a work of art—so—so *finished*!'

He went on:

'You know, I think ours will be the perfect marriage. . . . We both love each other enough and not too much. We're good friends. We've got a lot of tastes in common. We know each other through and through. We've all the advantages of cousinship without the disadvantages of blood relationship. I shall never get tired of you, because you're such an elusive creature. *You* may get tired of *me*, though. I'm such an ordinary sort of chap——'

Elinor shook her head. She said:

'I shan't get tired of you, Roddy—never.'

'My sweet!'

He kissed her.

He said:

'Aunt Laura has a pretty shrewd idea of how it is with us, I think, although we haven't been down since we finally fixed it up. It rather gives us an excuse, doesn't it, for going down?'

'Yes. I was thinking the other day——'

Roddy finished the sentence for her:

'—That we hadn't been down as often as we might. I thought that, too. When she first had her stroke we went down almost every other week-end. And now it must be almost two months since we were there.'

Elinor said:

'We'd have gone if she'd asked for us—at once.'

'Yes, of course. And we know that she likes Nurse O'Brien and is well looked after. All the same, perhaps we *have* been a bit slack. I'm talking now not from the money point of view —but the sheer human one.'

Elinor nodded.

'I know.'

'So that filthy letter has done some good, after all! We'll go down to protect our interests *and* because we're fond of the old dear!'

He lit a match and set fire to the letter which he took from Elinor's hand.

'Wonder who wrote it?' he said. 'Not that it matters. . . . Someone who was "on our side," as we used to say when we

16

were kids. Perhaps they've done us a good turn, too. Jim Partington's mother went out to the Riviera to live, had a handsome young Italian doctor to attend her, became quite crazy about him and left him every penny she had. Jim and his sisters tried to upset the will, but couldn't.'

Elinor said:

'Aunt Laura likes the new doctor who's taken over Dr. Ransome's practice—but not to that extent! Anyway, that horrid letter mentioned a girl. It must be Mary.'

Roddy said:

'We'll go down and see for ourselves. . . .'

II

Nurse O'Brien rustled out of Mrs. Welman's bedroom and into the bathroom. She said over her shoulder:

'I'll just pop the kettle on. You could do with a cup of tea before you go on, I'm sure, Nurse.'

Nurse Hopkins said comfortably:

'Well, dear, I can *always* do with a cup of tea. I always say there's nothing like a nice cup of tea—a strong cup!'

Nurse O'Brien said as she filled the kettle and lit the gas-ring:

'I've got everything here in this cupboard—teapot and cups and sugar—and Edna brings me up fresh milk twice a day. No need to be forever ringing bells. 'Tis a fine gas-ring, this; boils a kettle in a flash.'

Nurse O'Brien was a tall red-haired woman of thirty with flashing white teeth, a freckled face and an engaging smile. Her cheerfulness and vitality made her a favourite with her patients. Nurse Hopkins, the District Nurse who came every morning to assist with the bed-making and toilet of the heavy old lady, was a homely-looking middle-aged woman with a capable air and a brisk manner.

She said now approvingly:

'Everything's very well done in this house.'

The other nodded.

'Yes, old-fashioned, some of it, no central heating, but plenty of fires and all the maids are very obliging girls and Mrs. Bishop looks after them well.'

Nurse Hopkins said:

'These girls nowadays—I've no patience with 'em—don't

know what they want, most of them—and can't do a decent day's work.'

'Mary Gerrard's a nice girl,' said Nurse O'Brien. 'I really don't know what Mrs. Welman would do without her. You saw how she asked for her now? Ah, well, she's a lovely creature, I will say, and she's got a way with her.'

Nurse Hopkins said:

'I'm sorry for Mary. That old father of hers does his best to spite the girl.'

'Not a civil word in his head, the old curmudgeon,' said Nurse O'Brien. 'There, the kettle's singing. I'll wet the tea as soon as it comes to the boil.'

The tea was made and poured, hot and strong. The two nurses sat with it in Nurse O'Brien's room next door to Mrs. Welman's bedroom.

'Mr. Welman and Miss Carlisle are coming down,' said Nurse O'Brien. 'There was a telegram came this morning.'

'There now, dear,' said Nurse Hopkins. 'I thought the old lady was looking excited about something. It's some time since they've been down, isn't it?'

'It must be two months and over. Such a nice young gentleman, Mr. Welman. But very proud-looking.'

Nurse Hopkins said:

'I saw *her* picture in the *Tatler* the other day—with a friend at Newmarket.'

Nurse O'Brien said:

'She's very well known in society, isn't she? And always has such lovely clothes. Do you think she's really good-looking, Nurse?'

Nurse Hopkins said:

'Difficult to tell what these girls really look like under their make-up! In my opinion, she hasn't got anything like the looks Mary Gerrard has!'

Nurse O'Brien pursed her lips and put her head on one side.

'You may be right now. But Mary hasn't got the *style*!'

Nurse Hopkins said sententiously:

'Fine feathers make fine birds.'

'Another cup of tea, Nurse?'

'Thank you, Nurse. I don't mind if I do.'

Over their steaming cups the women drew a little closer together.

Nurse O'Brien said:

'An odd thing happened last night. I went in at two o'clock

18

to settle my dear comfortably, as I always do, and she was lying there awake. But she must have been dreaming, for as soon as I got into the room she said, "The photograph. I must have the photograph."

'So I said, "Why, of course, Mrs. Welman. But wouldn't you rather wait till morning?" And she said, "No, I want to look at it now." So I said, "Well, where *is* this photograph? Is it the one of Mr. Roderick you're meaning?" And she said, "Roder-ick? No. *Lewis.*" And she began to struggle, and I went to lift her and she got out her keys from the little box beside her bed and told me to unlock the second drawer of the tall-boy, and there, sure enough, was a big photograph in a silver frame. *Such* a handsome man. And "*Lewis*" written across the corner. Old-fashioned, of course, must have been taken many years ago. I took it to her and she held it there, staring at it a long time. And she just murmured. "*Lewis—Lewis.*" Then she sighed and gave it to me and told me to put it back. And, would you believe it, when I turned round again she'd gone off as sweetly as a child.'

Nurse Hopkins said:

'Was it her husband, do you think?'

Nurse O'Brien said:

'It was not! For this morning I asked Mrs. Bishop, careless-like, what was the late Mr. Welman's first name, and it was Henry, she told me!'

The two women exchanged glances. Nurse Hopkins had a long nose, and the end of it quivered a little with pleasurable emotion. She said thoughtfully:

'Lewis—Lewis. I wonder, now. I don't recall the name anywhere round these parts.'

'It would be many years ago, dear,' the other reminded her.

'Yes, and, of course, I've only been here a couple of years. I wonder now——'

Nurse O'Brien said:

'A *very* handsome man. Looked as though he might be a cavalry officer!'

Nurse Hopkins sipped her tea. She said:

'That's very interesting.'

Nurse O'Brien said romantically:

'Maybe they were boy and girl together and a cruel father separated them. . . .'

Nurse Hopkins said with a deep sigh:

'Perhaps he was killed in the war. . . .'

When Nurse Hopkins, pleasantly stimulated by tea and romantic speculation, finally left the house, Mary Gerrard ran out of the door to overtake her.

'Oh, Nurse, may I walk down to the village with you?'

'Of course you can, Mary, my dear.'

Mary Gerrard said breathlessly:

'I *must* talk to you. I'm so worried about everything.'

The older woman looked at her kindly.

At twenty-one, Mary Gerrard was a lovely creature with a kind of wild-rose unreality about her: a long delicate neck, pale golden hair lying close to her exquisitely shaped head in soft natural waves, and eyes of a deep vivid blue.

Nurse Hopkins said:

'What's the trouble?'

'The trouble is that the time is going on and on and I'm not *doing* anything!'

Nurse Hopkins said dryly:

'Time enough for that.'

'No, but it is so—so unsettling. Mrs. Welman has been wonderfully kind, giving me all that expensive schooling. I do feel now that I ought to be starting to earn my own living. I ought to be training for something.'

Nurse Hopkins nodded sympathetically.

'It's such a waste of everything if I don't. I've tried to—to explain what I feel to Mrs. Welman, but—it's difficult—she doesn't seem to understand. She keeps saying there's plenty of time.'

Nurse Hopkins said:

'She's a sick woman, remember.'

Mary flushed, a contrite flush.

'Oh, I know. I suppose I oughtn't to bother her. But it *is* worrying—and Father's so—so *beastly* about it! Keeps jibing at me for being a fine lady! But indeed *I* don't want to sit about doing nothing!'

'I know you don't.'

'The trouble is that training of any kind is nearly always expensive. I know German pretty well now, and I might do something with that. But I think really I want to be a hospital nurse. I do like nursing and sick people.'

Nurse Hopkins said unromantically:

'You've got to be as strong as a horse, remember!'

'I am strong! And I really *do* like nursing. Mother's sister, the one in New Zealand, was a nurse. So it's in my blood, you see.'

'What about massage?' suggested Nurse Hopkins. 'Or Norland? You're fond of children. There's good money to be made in massage.'

Mary said doubtfully:

'It's expensive to train for it, isn't it? I hoped—but of course that's very greedy of me—she's done so much for me already.'

'Mrs. Welman, you mean? Nonsense. In my opinion, she owes you that. She's given you a slap-up education, but not the kind that leads to anything much. You don't want to teach?'

'I'm not clever enough.'

Nurse Hopkins said:

'There's brains and brains! If you take my advice, Mary, you'll be patient for the present. In my opinion, as I said, Mrs. Welman owes it to you to help you get a start at making your living. And I've no doubt she means to do it. But the truth of the matter is, she's got fond of you, and she doesn't want to lose you.'

Mary said:

'Oh!' She drew in her breath with a little gasp. 'Do you really think that's it?'

'I haven't the least doubt of it! There she is, poor old lady, more or less helpless, paralysed one side and nothing and nobody much to amuse her. It means a lot to her to have a fresh, pretty young thing like you about the house. You've a very nice way with you in a sick-room.'

Mary said softly:

'If you really think so—that makes me feel better. . . . Dear Mrs. Welman, I'm very, *very* fond of her! She's been so good to me always. I'd do *anything* for her!'

Nurse Hopkins said dryly:

'Then the best thing you can do is to stay where you are and stop worrying! It won't be for long.'

Mary said, 'Do you mean——?'

Her eyes looked wide and frightened.

The District Nurse nodded.

'She's rallied wonderfully, but it won't be for long. There will be a second stroke and then a third. I know the way of it only too well. You be patient, my dear. If you keep the old

21

lady's last days happy and occupied, that's a better deed than many. The time for the other will come.'

Mary said:

'You're very kind.'

Nurse Hopkins said:

'Here's your father coming out from the lodge—and not to pass the time of day pleasantly, I should say!'

They were just nearing the big iron gates. On the steps of the lodge an elderly man with a bent back was painfully hobbling down the two steps.

Nurse Hopkins said cheerfully:

'Good-morning, Mr. Gerrard.'

Ephraim Gerrard said crustily:

'Ah!'

'Very nice weather,' said Nurse Hopkins.

Old Gerrard said crossly:

'May be for you. 'Tisn't for me. My lumbago's been at me something cruel.'

Nurse Hopkins said cheerfully:

'That was the wet spell last week, I expect. This hot dry weather will soon clear *that* away.'

Her brisk professional manner appeared to annoy the old man.

He said disagreeably:

'Nurses—nurses, you'm all the same. Full of cheerfulness over other people's troubles. Little *you* care! And there's Mary talks about being a nurse, too. Should have thought she'd want to be something better than *that*, with her French and her German and her piano-playing and all the things she's learned at her grand school and her travels abroad.'

Mary said sharply:

'Being a hospital nurse would be quite good enough for me!'

'Yes, and you'd sooner do nothing at all, wouldn't you? Strutting about with your airs and your graces and your fine-lady-do-nothing ways. Laziness, that's what *you* like, my girl!'

Mary protested, tears springing to her eyes:

'It isn't true, Dad. You've no right to say that!'

Nurse Hopkins intervened with a heavy, determinedly humorous air.

'Just a bit under the weather, aren't we, this morning? You don't really mean what you say, Gerrard. Mary's a good girl and a good daughter to you.'

Gerrard looked at his daughter with an air of almost active malevolence.

'She's no daughter of mine—nowadays—with her French and her history and her mincing talk. Pah!'

He turned and went into the lodge again.

Mary said, the tears still standing in her eyes:

'You do see, Nurse, don't you, how difficult it is? He's so unreasonable. He's never really liked me even when I was a little girl. Mum was always standing up for me.'

Nurse Hopkins said kindly:

'There, there, don't worry. These things are sent to try us! Goodness, I must hurry. Such a round as I've got this morning.'

And as she stood watching the brisk retreating figure, Mary Gerrard thought forlornly that nobody was any real good or could really help you. Nurse Hopkins, for all her kindness, was quite content to bring out a little stock of platitudes and offer them with an air of novelty.

Mary thought disconsolately:

'What *shall* I do?'

CHAPTER TWO

I

Mrs. Welman lay on her carefully built-up pillows. Her breathing was a little heavy, but she was not asleep. Her eyes—eyes still deep and blue like those of her niece Elinor, looked up at the ceiling. She was a big, heavy woman, with a handsome, hawk-like profile. Pride and determination showed in her face.

The eyes dropped and came to rest on the figure sitting by the window. They rested there tenderly—almost wistfully.

She said at last:

'Mary——'

The girl turned quickly.

'Oh, you're awake, Mrs. Welman.'

Laura Welman said:

'Yes, I've been awake some time. . . .'

'Oh, I didn't know. I'd have——'

Mrs. Welman broke in:

'No, that's all right. I was thinking—thinking of many things.'

'Yes, Mrs. Welman?'

The sympathetic look, the interested voice, made a tender look come into the older woman's face. She said gently:

'I'm very fond of you, my dear. You're very good to me.'

'Oh, Mrs. Welman, it's *you* who have been good to *me*. If it hadn't been for you, I don't know what I should have done! You've done *everything* for me.'

'I don't know . . . I don't know, I'm sure. . . .' The sick woman moved restlessly, her right arm twitched—the left remaining inert and lifeless. 'One means to do the best one can; but it's so difficult to know what is best—what is *right*. I've been too sure of myself always. . . .'

Mary Gerrard said:

'Oh, no, I'm sure you *always* know what is best and right to do.'

But Laura Welman shook her head.

'No—no. It worries me. I've had one besetting sin always, Mary: I'm proud. Pride can be the devil. It runs in our family. Elinor has it, too.'

Mary said quickly:

'It will be nice for you to have Miss Elinor and Mr. Roderick down. It will cheer you up a lot. It's quite a time since they were here.'

Mrs. Welman said softly:

'They're good children—very good children. And fond of me, both of them. I always know I've only got to send and they'll come at any time. But I don't want to do that too often. They're young and happy—the world in front of them. No need to bring them near decay and suffering before their time.'

Mary said, 'I'm sure they'd *never* feel like that, Mrs. Welman.'

Mrs. Welman went on, talking perhaps more to herself than to the girl:

'I always hoped they might marry. But I tried never to suggest anything of the kind. Young people are so contradictory. It would have put them off! I had an idea, long ago when they were children, that Elinor had set her heart on Roddy. But I wasn't at all sure about *him*. He's a funny creature. Henry was like that—very reserved and fastidious. . . . Yes, Henry. . . .'

She was silent for a little, thinking of her dead husband. She murmured:

'So long ago . . . so very long ago. . . . We had only been married five years when he died. Double pneumonia. . . . We were happy—yes, very happy; but somehow it all seems very *unreal*, that happiness. I was an odd, solemn, undeveloped girl—my head full of ideas and hero-worship. No *reality*. . . .'

Mary murmured:

'You must have been very lonely—afterwards.'

'After? Oh, yes—terribly lonely. I was twenty-six . . . and now I'm over sixty. A long time, my dear . . . a long, long time. . . .' She said with sudden brisk acerbity, 'And now *this*!'

'Your illness?'

'Yes. A stroke is the thing I've always dreaded. The indignity of it all! Washed and tended like a baby! Helpless to do anything for yourself. It maddens me. The O'Brien creature is good-natured—I will say that for her. She doesn't mind my snapping at her and she's not more idiotic than most of them. But it makes a lot of difference to me to have *you* about, Mary.'

'Does it?' The girl flushed. 'I—I'm so glad, Mrs. Welman.'

Laura Welman said shrewdly:

'You've been worrying, haven't you? About the future. You leave it to me, my dear. I'll see to it that you shall have the means to be independent and take up a profession. But be patient for a little—it means too much to me to have you here.'

'Oh, Mrs. Welman, of course—of *course*! I wouldn't leave you for the world. Not if you want me——'

'I do want you . . .' The voice was unusually deep and full. 'You're—you're quite like a daughter to me, Mary. I've seen you grow up here at Hunterbury from a little toddling thing—seen you grow into a beautiful girl. . . . I'm proud of you, child. I only hope I've done what was best for you.'

Mary said quickly:

'If you mean that your having been so good to me and having educated me above—well, above my station—if you think it's made me dissatisfied or—or—given me what Father calls fine-lady ideas, indeed that isn't true. I'm just ever so grateful, that's all. And if I'm anxious to start earning my living, it's only because I feel it's right that I should, and not —and not—well, do nothing after all you've done for me. I—I shouldn't like it to be thought that I was sponging on you.'

25

Laura Welman said, and her voice was suddenly sharp-edged:

'So that's what Gerrard's been putting into your head? Pay no attention to your father, Mary; there never has been and never will be any question of your sponging on me! I'm asking you to stay here a little longer solely on my account. Soon it will be over. . . . If they went the proper way about things, my life could be ended here and now—none of this long-drawn-out tomfoolery with nurses and doctors.'

'Oh, no, Mrs. Welman, Dr. Lord says you may live for years.'

'I'm not at all anxious to, thank you! I told him the other day that in a decently civilised state, all there would be to do would be for me to intimate to him that I wished to end it, and he'd finish me off painlessly with some nice drug. "And if you'd any courage, Doctor," I said, "you'd do it, anyway!"'

Mary cried:

'Oh! What did he say?'

'The disrespectful young man merely grinned at me, my dear, and said he wasn't going to risk being hanged. He said, "If you'd left me all your money, Mrs. Welman, that would be different, of course!" Impudent young jackanapes! But I like him. His visits do me more good than his medicines.'

'Yes, he's very nice,' said Mary. 'Nurse O'Brien thinks a lot of him and so does Nurse Hopkins.'

Mrs. Welman said:

'Hopkins ought to have more sense at her age. As for O'Brien, she simpers and says, "Oh, doctor," and tosses those long streamers of hers whenever he comes near her.'

'Poor Nurse O'Brien.'

Mrs. Welman said indulgently:

'She's not a bad sort, really, but all nurses annoy me; they always will think that you'd like "a nice cup of tea" at five in the morning!' She paused. 'What's that? Is it the car?'

Mary looked out of the window.

'Yes, it's the car. Miss Elinor and Mr. Roderick have arrived.'

Mrs. Welman said to her niece:

'I'm very glad, Elinor, about you and Roddy.'

Elinor smiled at her.

'I thought you would be, Aunt Laura.'

The older woman said, after a moment's hesitation:

'You do—care about him, Elinor?'

Elinor's delicate brows lifted.

'Of course.'

Laura Welman said quickly:

'You must forgive me, dear. You know, you're very reserved. It's very difficult to know what you're thinking or feeling. When you were both much younger I thought you were perhaps beginning to care for Roddy—too much. . . .'

Again Elinor's delicate brows were raised.

'Too much?'

The older woman nodded.

'Yes. It's not wise to care too much. Sometimes a very young girl does do just that. . . . I was glad when you went abroad to Germany to finish. Then, when you came back, you seemed quite indifferent to him—and, well, I was sorry for that, too! I'm a tiresome old woman, difficult to satisfy! But I've always fancied that you had, perhaps, rather an intense nature—that kind of temperament runs in our family. It isn't a very happy one for its possessors. . . . But, as I say, when you came back from abroad so indifferent to Roddy, I was sorry about that, because I had always hoped you two would come together. And now you have, and so everything is all right! And you *do* really care for him?'

Elinor said gravely:

'I care for Roddy enough and not too much.'

Mrs. Welman nodded approval.

'I think, then, you'll be happy. Roddy needs love—but he doesn't like violent emotion. He'd shy off from possessiveness.'

Elinor said with feeling:

'You know Roddy very well!'

Mrs. Welman said:

'If Roddy cares for you just a *little* more than you care for him—well, that's all to the good.'

Elinor said sharply:

'Aunt Agatha's Advice Column. *"Keep your boy friend guessing! Don't let him be too sure of you!"*'

Laura Welman said sharply:

'Are you unhappy, child? Is anything wrong?'

'No, no, nothing.'

Laura Welman said:

'You just thought I was being rather—cheap? My dear, you're young and sensitive. Life, I'm afraid, *is* rather cheap. . . .'

Elinor said with some slight bitterness:

'I suppose it is.'

Laura Welman said:

'My child—you *are* unhappy? What is it?'

'Nothing—absolutely nothing.' She got up and went to the window. Half turning, she said:

'Aunt Laura, tell me, honestly, do you think love is ever a happy thing?'

Mrs. Welman's face became grave.

'In the sense you mean, Elinor—no, probably not. . . . To care passionately for another human creature brings always more sorrow than joy; but all the same, Elinor, one would not be without that experience. Anyone who has never really loved has never really lived. . . .'

The girl nodded.

She said:

'Yes—you understand—you've known what it's like——'

She turned suddenly, a questioning look in her eyes:

'Aunt Laura——'

The door opened and red-haired Nurse O'Brien came in.

She said in a sprightly manner:

'Mrs. Welman, here's Doctor come to see you.'

III

Dr. Lord was a young man of thirty-two. He had sandy hair, a pleasantly ugly freckled face and a remarkably square jaw. His eyes were a keen, piercing light blue.

'Good-morning, Mrs. Welman,' he said.

'Good-morning, Dr. Lord. This is my niece, Miss Carlisle.'

A very obvious admiration sprang into Dr. Lord's transparent face. He said, 'How do you do?' The hand that Elinor extended to him he took rather gingerly as though he thought he might break it.

Mrs. Welman went on:

'Elinor and my nephew have come down to cheer me up.'

'Splendid!' said Dr. Lord. 'Just what you need! It will do you a lot of good, I am sure, Mrs. Welman.'

He was still looking at Elinor with obvious admiration.

Elinor said, moving towards the door:

'Perhaps I shall see you before you go, Dr. Lord?'

'Oh—er—yes, of course.'

She went out, shutting the door behind her. Dr. Lord approached the bed, Nurse O'Brien fluttering behind him.

Mrs. Welman said with a twinkle:

'Going through the usual bag of tricks, Doctor: pulse, respiration, temperature? What humbugs you doctors are!'

Nurse O'Brien said with a sigh:

'Oh, Mrs. Welman. What a thing, now, to be saying to the doctor!'

Dr. Lord said with a twinkle:

'Mrs. Welman sees through me, Nurse! All the same, Mrs. Welman, I've got to do my stuff, you know. The trouble with me is I've never learnt the right bedside manner.'

'Your bedside manner's all right. Actually you're rather proud of it.'

Peter Lord chuckled and remarked:

'That's what *you* say.'

After a few routine questions had been asked and answered, Dr. Lord leant back in his chair and smiled at his patient.

'Well,' he said. 'You're going on splendidly.'

Laura Welman said: 'So I shall be up and walking round the house in a few weeks' time?'

'Not quite so quickly as that.'

'No, indeed. You humbug! What's the good of living stretched out like this, and cared for like a baby?'

Dr. Lord said:

'What's the good of life, anyway? That's the real question. Ever read about that nice mediæval invention, the Little Ease? You couldn't stand, sit or lie in it. You'd think anyone condemned to that would die in a few weeks. Not at all. One man lived for sixteen years in an iron cage, was released and lived to a hearty old age.'

Laura Welman said:

'What's the point of this story?'

Peter Lord said:

'The point is that one's got an *instinct* to live. One doesn't live because one's *reason* assents to living. People who, as we say, "would be better dead," don't want to die! People who apparently have got everything to live for just let themselves fade out of life because they haven't got the energy to fight.'

'Go on.'

'There's nothing more. You're one of the people who really *want* to live, whatever you say about it! And if your body wants to live, it's no good your brain dishing out the other stuff.'

Mrs. Welman said with an abrupt change of subject:

'How do you like it down here?'

Peter Lord said, smiling:

'It suits me fine.'

'Isn't it a bit irksome for a young man like you? Don't you want to specialise? Don't you find a country G.P. practice rather boring?'

Lord shook his sandy head.

'No, I like my job. I like *people*, you know, and I like ordinary everyday diseases. I don't really want to pin down the rare bacillus of an obscure disease. I like measles and chicken-pox and all the rest of it. I like seeing how different bodies react to them. I like seeing if I can't improve on recognised treatment. The trouble with me is I've got absolutely no ambition. I shall stay here till I grow side-whiskers and people begin saying, "Of course, we've always had Dr. Lord, and he's a nice old man; but he *is* very old-fashioned in his methods and perhaps we'd better call in young so-and-so, who's so very up to date. . . ." '

'H'm,' said Mrs. Welman. 'You seem to have got it all taped out!'

Peter Lord got up.

'Well,' he said. 'I must be off.'

Mrs. Welman said:

'My niece will want to speak to you, I expect. By the way, what do you think of her? You haven't seen her before.'

Dr. Lord went suddenly scarlet. His very eyebrows blushed. He said:

'I—oh! she's very good-looking, isn't she? And—eh—clever and all that, I should think.'

Mrs. Welman was diverted. She thought to herself:

'How very young he is, really. . . .'

Aloud she said:
'You ought to get married.'

IV

Roddy had wandered into the garden. He had crossed the
broad sweep of lawn and along a paved walk and had then
entered the walled kitchen-garden. It was well-kept and well-
stocked. He wondered if he and Elinor would live at Hunterbury one day. He supposed that they would. He himself would
like that. He preferred country life. He was a little doubtful
about Elinor. Perhaps she'd like living in London better. . . .

A little difficult to know where you were with Elinor. She
didn't reveal much of what she thought and felt about things.
He liked that about her. . . . He hated people who reeled off
their thoughts and feelings to you, who took it for granted
that you wanted to know all their inner mechanism. Reserve
was always more interesting.

Elinor, he thought judicially, was really quite perfect. Nothing about her ever jarred or offended. She was delightful to
look at, witty to talk to—altogether the most charming of
companions.

He thought complacently to himself:

'I'm damned lucky to have got her. Can't think what she
sees in a chap like me.'

For Roderick Welman, in spite of his fastidiousness, was not
conceited. It did honestly strike him as strange that Elinor
should have consented to marry him.

Life stretched ahead of him pleasantly enough. One knew
pretty well where one was; that was always a blessing. He
supposed that Elinor and he would be married quite soon—
that is, if Elinor wanted to; perhaps she'd rather put it off for
a bit. He mustn't rush her. They'd be a bit hard-up at first.
Nothing to worry about, though. He hoped sincerely that Aunt
Laura wouldn't die for a long time to come. She was a dear
and had always been nice to him, having him there for holidays, always interested in what he was doing.

His mind shied away from the thought of her actual death
(his mind usually did shy away from any concrete unpleasantness). He didn't like to visualise anything unpleasant too
clearly. . . . But—er—afterwards—well, it would be very
pleasant to live here, especially as there would be plenty of

31

money to keep it up. He wondered exactly how his aunt had left it. Not that it really mattered. With some women it would matter a good deal whether husband or wife had the money. But not with Elinor. She had plenty of tact and she didn't care enough about money to make too much of it.

He thought: 'No, there's nothing to worry about—whatever happens!'

He went out of the walled garden by the gate at the far end. From there he wandered into the little wood where the daffodils were in spring. They were over now, of course. But the green light was very lovely where the sunlight came filtering through the trees.

Just for a moment an odd restlessness came to him—a rippling of his previous placidity. He felt: 'There's something—something I haven't got—something I want—I want—I want. . . .'

The golden green light, the softness in the air—with them came a quickened pulse, a stirring of the blood, a sudden impatience.

A girl came through the trees towards him—a girl with pale, gleaming hair and a rose-flushed skin.

He thought, 'How beautiful—how unutterably beautiful.'

Something gripped him; he stood quite still, as though frozen into immobility. The world, he felt, was spinning, was topsy-turvy, was suddenly and impossibly and gloriously crazy!

The girl stopped suddenly, then she came on. She came up to him where he stood, dumb and absurdly fish-like, his mouth open.

She said with a little hesitation:

'Don't you remember me, Mr Roderick? It's a long time, of course. I'm Mary Gerrard, from the Lodge.'

Roddy said:

'Oh—oh—you're Mary Gerrard?'

She said: 'Yes.'

Then she went on rather shyly:

'I've changed, of course, since you saw me.'

He said: 'Yes, you've changed. I—I wouldn't have recognised you.'

He stood staring at her. He did not hear footsteps behind him. Mary did and turned.

Elinor stood motionless a minute. Then she said:

'Hallo, Mary.'

Mary said:

'How do you do, Miss Elinor? It's nice to see you. Mrs. Welman has been looking forward to you coming down.'

Elinor said:

'Yes—it's a long time. I—Nurse O'Brien sent me to look for you. She wants to lift Mrs. Welman up, and she says you usually do it with her.'

Mary said: 'I'll go at once.'

She moved off, breaking into a run. Elinor stood looking after her. Mary ran well, grace in every movement.

Roddy said softly: 'Atalanta . . .'

Elinor did not answer. She stood quite still for a minute or two. Then she said:

'It's nearly lunch-time. We'd better go back.'

They walked side by side towards the house.

V

'Oh! Come on, Mary. It's Garbo, and a grand film—all about Paris. And a story by a tiptop author. There was an opera of it once.'

'It's frightfully nice of you, Ted, but I really won't.'

Ted Bigland said angrily:

'I can't make you out nowadays, Mary. You're different—altogether different.'

'No, I'm not, Ted.'

'You are! I suppose because you've been away to that grand school and to Germany. You're too good for us now.'

'It's not true, Ted. I'm not like that.'

She spoke vehemently.

The young man, a fine sturdy specimen, looked at her appraisingly in spite of his anger.

'Yes, you are. You're almost a lady, Mary.'

Mary said with sudden bitterness:

'Almost isn't much good, is it?'

He said with sudden understanding:

'No, I reckon it isn't.'

Mary said quickly:

'Anyway, who cares about that sort of thing nowadays? Ladies and gentlemen, and all that!'

'It doesn't matter like it did—no,' Ted assented, but thoughtfully. 'All the same, there's a *feeling*. Lord, Mary, you *look* like a duchess or a countess or something.'

Mary said:

'That's not saying much. I've seen countesses looking like old-clothes women!'

'Well, you know what I mean.'

A stately figure of ample proportions, handsomely dressed in black, bore down upon them. Her eyes gave them a sharp glance. Ted moved aside a step or two. He said:

'Afternoon, Mrs. Bishop.'

Mrs. Bishop inclined her head graciously.

'Good-afternoon, Ted Bigland. Good-afternoon, Mary.'

She passed on, a ship in full sail.

Ted looked respectfully after her.

Mary murmured:

'Now, she really is like a duchess!'

'Yes—she's got a manner. Always makes me feel hot inside my collar.'

Mary said slowly:

'She doesn't like me.'

'Nonsense, my girl.'

'It's true. She doesn't. She's always saying sharp things to me.'

'Jealous,' said Ted, nodding his head sapiently. 'That's all it is.'

Mary said doubtfully:

'I suppose it might be that. . . .'

'That's it, depend upon it. She's been housekeeper at Hunterbury for years, ruling the roost and ordering everyone about, and now old Mrs. Welman takes a fancy to you, and it puts her out! That's all it is.'

Mary said, a shade of trouble on her forehead:

'It's silly of me, but I can't bear it when anyone doesn't like me. I want people to like me.'

'Sure to be women who don't like you, Mary! Jealous cats who think you're too good-looking!'

Mary said:

'I think jealousy's horrible.'

Ted said slowly:

'Maybe—*but it exists all right*. Say, I saw a lovely film over at Alledore last week. Clark Gable. All about one of these millionaire blokes who neglected his wife; and then she pretended she'd done the dirty on him. And there was another fellow . . .'

Mary moved away. She said:

'Sorry, Ted, I must go. I'm late.'

'Where are you going?'

'I'm going to have tea with Nurse Hopkins.'

Ted made a face.

'Funny taste. That woman's the biggest gossip in the village! Pokes that long nose of hers into everything.'

Mary said:

'She's been very kind to me always.'

'Oh, I'm not saying there's any harm in her. But she talks.'

Mary said:

'Good-bye, Ted.'

She hurried off, leaving him standing gazing resentfully after her.

VI

Nurse Hopkins occupied a small cottage at the end of the village. She herself had just come in and was untying her bonnet strings when Mary entered.

'Ah, there you are. I'm a bit late. Old Mrs. Caldecott was bad again. Made me late with my round of dressings. I saw you with Ted Bigland at the end of the street.'

Mary said rather dispiritedly:

'Yes . . .'

Nurse Hopkins looked up alertly from where she was stooping to light the gas-ring under the kettle.

Her long nose twitched.

'Was he saying something particular to you, my dear?'

'No. He just asked me to go to the cinema.'

'*I* see,' said Nurse Hopkins promptly. 'Well, of course, he's a nice young fellow and doesn't do too badly at the garage, and his father does rather better than most of the farmers round here. All the same, my dear, you don't seem to me cut out for Ted Bigland's wife. Not with your education and all. As I was saying, if I was you I'd go in for massage when the time comes. You get about a bit and see people that way; and your time's more or less your own.'

Mary said:

'I'll think it over. Mrs. Welman spoke to me the other day. She was very sweet about it. It was just exactly as you said it was. She doesn't want me to go away just now. She'd miss me,

35

she said. But she told me not to worry about the future, that she meant to help me.'

Nurse Hopkins said dubiously:

'Let's hope she's put that down in black and white! Sick people are odd.'

Mary asked:

'Do you think Mrs. Bishop really dislikes me—or is it only my fancy?'

Nurse Hopkins considered a minute.

'She puts on a sour face, I must say. She's one of those who don't like seeing young people having a good time or anything done for them. Thinks, perhaps, Mrs. Welman is a bit too fond of you, and resents it.'

She laughed cheerfully.

'I shouldn't worry if I was you, Mary, my dear. Just open that paper bag, will you? There's a couple of doughnuts in it.'

CHAPTER THREE

I

Your Aunt had second stroke last night No cause immediate anxiety but suggest you should come down if possible Lord.

II

Immediately on receipt of the telegram Elinor had rung up Roddy, and now they were in the train together bound for Hunterbury.

Elinor had not seen much of Roddy in the week that had elapsed since their visit. On the two brief occasions when they had met, there had been an odd kind of constraint between them. Roddy had sent her flowers—a great sheaf of long-stemmed roses. It was unusual on his part. At a dinner they had had together he had seemed more attentive than usual, consulting her preferences in food and drink, being unusually assiduous in helping her on and off with her coat. A little, Elinor thought, as though he were playing a part in a play—the part of the devoted fiancé. . . .

Then she had said to herself:

'Don't be an idiot. Nothing's wrong. . . . You imagine things! It's that beastly brooding, possessive mind of yours.'

Her manner to him had been perhaps a shade more detached, more aloof than usual.

Now, in this sudden emergency, the constraint passed, they talked together naturally enough.

Roddy said:

'Poor old dear, and she was so well when we saw her the other day.'

Elinor said:

'I do mind so terribly for *her*. I know how she hated being ill, anyway, and now I suppose she'll be more helpless still, and she'll simply loathe that! One does feel, Roddy, that people ought to be set free—if they themselves really want it.'

Roddy said:

'I agree. It's the only civilised thing to do. You put animals out of their pain. I suppose you don't do it with human beings simply because, human nature being what it is, people would get shoved off for their money by their fond relations—perhaps when they weren't really bad at all.'

Elinor said thoughtfully:

'It would be in the doctors' hands, of course.'

'A doctor might be a crook.'

'You could trust a man like Dr. Lord.'

Roddy said carelessly:

'Yes, he seems straightforward enough. Nice fellow.'

III

Dr. Lord was leaning over the bed. Nurse O'Brien hovered behind him. He was trying, his forehead puckered, to understand the slurred sounds coming from his patient's mouth.

He said:

'Yes, yes. Now, don't get excited. Take plenty of time. Just raise this right hand a little when you mean *yes*. There's something you're worried about?'

He received the affirmatory sign.

'Something urgent? Yes. Something you want *done*? Someone sent for? Miss Carlisle? And Mr. Welman? They're on their way.'

Again Mrs. Welman tried incoherently to speak. Dr. Lord listened attentively.

'You wanted them to come, but it's not that? Someone else? A relation? No? Some business matter? I see. Something to do with money? *Lawyer*? That's right, isn't it You want to see your lawyer? Want to give him instructions about something?

'Now, now—that's all right. Keep calm. Plenty of time. What's that you're saying—Elinor?' He caught the garbled name. 'She knows what lawyer? And she will arrange with him? Good. She'll be here in about half an hour. I'll tell her what you want and I'll come up with her and we'll get it all straight. Now, don't worry any more. Leave it all to me. I'll see that things are arranged the way you want them to be.'

He stood a moment watching her relax, then he moved quietly away and went out on the landing. Nurse O'Brien followed him. Nurse Hopkins was just coming up the stairs. He nodded to her. She said breathlessly:

'Good-evening, Doctor.'

'Good-evening, Nurse.'

He went with the two of them into Nurse O'Brien's room next door and gave them their instructions. Nurse Hopkins would remain on overnight and take charge with Nurse O'Brien.

'To-morrow I'll have to get hold of a second resident nurse. Awkward, this diphtheria epidemic over at Stamford. The nursing homes there are working short-handed as it is.'

Then, having given his orders, which were listened to with reverent attention (which sometimes tickled him), Dr. Lord went downstairs, ready to receive the niece and nephew who, his watch told him, were due to arrive at any minute now.

In the hall he encountered Mary Gerrard. Her face was pale and anxious. She asked:

'Is she better?'

Dr. Lord said:

'I can ensure her a peaceful night—that's about all that can be done.'

Mary said brokenly:

'It seems so cruel—so unfair——'

He nodded sympathetically enough.

'Yes, it does seem like that sometimes. I believe——'

He broke off.

'That's the car.'

He went out into the hall. Mary ran upstairs.

Elinor exclaimed as she came into the drawing-room:]

'Is she very bad?'

Roddy was looking pale and apprehensive.

The doctor said gravely:

'I'm afraid it will be rather a shock to you. She's badly paralysed. Her speech is almost unrecognisable. By the way, she's definitely worried about something. It's to do with sending for her lawyer. You know who he is, Miss Carlisle?'

Elinor said quickly:

'Mr. Seddon—of Bloomsbury Square. But he wouldn't be there at this time of the evening, and I don't know his home address.'

Dr. Lord said reassuringly:

'To-morrow will be in plenty of time. But I'm anxious to set Mrs. Welman's mind at rest as soon as possible. If you will come up with me now Miss Carlisle, I think together we shall be able to reassure her.'

'Of course. I will come up at once.'

Roddy said hopefully:

'You don't want me?'

He felt faintly ashamed of himself, but he had a nervous dread of going up to the sick-room, of seeing Aunt Laura lying there inarticulate and helpless.

Dr. Lord reassured him promptly.

'Not the least need, Mr. Welman. Better not to have too many people in the room.'

Roddy's relief showed plainly.

Dr. Lord and Elinor went upstairs. Nurse O'Brien was with the patient.

Laura Welman, breathing deeply and stertorously, lay as though in a stupor. Elinor stood looking down on her, shocked by the drawn, twisted face.

Suddenly Mrs. Welman's right eyelid quivered and opened. A faint change came over her face as she recognised Elinor.

She tried to speak.

'*Elinor* . . .' The word would have been meaningless to any-one who had not guessed at what she wanted to say.

Elinor said quickly:

'I'm here, Aunt Laura. You're worried about something? You want me to send for Mr. Seddon?'

Another of those hoarse raucous sounds. Elinor guessed at the meaning. She said:

'Mary Gerrard?'

Slowly the right hand moved shakily in assent.

A long burble of sound came from the sick woman's lips.

Dr. Lord and Elinor frowned helplessly. Again and again it came. Then Elinor got a word.

'*Provision*? You want to make *provision* for her in your will? You want her to have some money? I see, dear Aunt Laura. That will be quite simple. Mr. Seddon will come down to-morrow and everything shall be arranged exactly as you wish.'

The sufferer seemed relieved. The look of distress faded from that appealing eye. Elinor took her hand in hers and felt a feeble pressure from the fingers.

Mrs. Welman said with a great effort:

'You—all—you . . .'

Elinor said:

'Yes, yes, leave it all to me. I will see that everything you want is done!'

She felt the pressure of the fingers again. Then it relaxed. The eyelids drooped and closed.

Dr. Lord laid a hand on Elinor's arm and drew her gently away out of the room. Nurse O'Brien resumed her seat near the bed.

Outside on the landing Mary Gerrard was talking to Nurse Hopkins. She started forward.

'Oh, Dr. Lord, can I go in to her, please?'

He nodded.

'Keep quite quiet, though, and don't disturb her.'

Mary went into the sick-room.

Dr. Lord said:

'Your train was late. You——' He stopped.

Elinor had turned her head to look after Mary. Suddenly she became aware of his abrupt silence. She turned her head and looked at him inquiringly. He was staring at her, a startled look in his face. The colour rose in Elinor's cheeks.

She said hurriedly:

'I beg your pardon. What did you say?'

Peter Lord said slowly:

'What was I saying? I don't remember. Miss Carlisle, you were splendid in there!' He spoke warmly. 'Quick to under-stand, reassuring, everything you should have been.'

The very faintest of sniffs came from Nurse Hopkins.

Elinor said:

'Poor darling. It upset me terribly seeing her like that.'

'Of course. But you didn't show it. You must have great self-control.'

Elinor said, her lips set very straight:

'I've learnt not—to show my feelings.'

The doctor said slowly:

'All the same the mask's bound to slip once in a while.'

Nurse Hopkins had bustled into the bathroom. Elinor said, raising her delicate eyebrows and looking full at him:

'The mask?'

Dr. Lord said:

'The human face is, after all, nothing more nor less than a mask.'

'And underneath?'

'Underneath is the primitive human man or woman.'

She turned away quickly and led the way downstairs.

Peter Lord followed, puzzled and unwontedly serious.

Roddy came out into the hall to meet them.

'Well?' he asked anxiously.

Elinor said:

'Poor darling. It's very sad to see her. . . . I shouldn't go, Roddy—till—till—she asks for you.'

Roddy asked:

'Did she want anything—special?'

Peter Lord said to Elinor:

'I must be off now. There's nothing more I can do for the moment. I'll look in early to-morrow. Good-bye, Miss Carlisle. Don't—don't worry too much.'

He held her hand in his for a moment or two. He had a strangely reassuring and comforting clasp. He looked at her, Elinor thought, rather oddly as though—as though he was sorry for her.

As the door shut behind the doctor, Roddy repeated his question.

Elinor said:

'Aunt Laura is worried about—about certain business matters. I managed to pacify her and told her Mr. Seddon would certainly come down to-morrow. We must telephone him first thing.'

Roddy asked:

'Does she want to make a new will?'

Elinor answered:

'She didn't say so.'

'What did she——?'

He stopped in the middle of the question.

Mary Gerrard was running down the stairs. She crossed the

41

hall and disappeared through the door to the kitchen quarters.

Elinor said in a harsh voice:

'Yes? What is it you wanted to ask?'

Roddy said vaguely:

'I—what? I've forgotten what it was.'

He was staring at the door through which Mary Gerrard had gone.

Elinor's hands closed. She could feel her long, pointed nails biting into the flesh of her palms.

She thought:

'I can't bear it—I can't bear it . . . it's not imagination . . . it's true . . . Roddy—Roddy I *can't* lose you . . .'

And she thought:

'What did that man—the doctor—*what did he see in my face upstairs?* He saw something. . . . Oh, God, how awful life is—to feel as I feel now. Say something, fool. Pull yourself together!'

Aloud she said, in her calm voice:

'About meals, Roddy. I'm not very hungry. I'll sit with Aunt Laura and the nurses can both come down.'

Roddy said in alarm:

'And have dinner with *me*?'

Elinor said coldly:

'They won't bite you!'

'But what about you? You must have something. Why don't *we* dine first, and let them come down afterwards?'

Elinor said:

'No, the other way's better.' She added wildly, 'They're so touchy, you know.'

She thought:

'*I can't sit through a meal with him—alone—talking—behaving as usual . . .*'

She said impatiently:

'Oh, do let me arrange things my own way!'

CHAPTER FOUR

I

It was no mere housemaid who wakened Elinor the following morning. It was Mrs. Bishop in person, rustling in her old-fashioned black, and weeping unashamedly.

'Oh, Miss Elinor, she's gone . . .'

'What?'

Elinor sat up in bed.

'Your dear aunt. Mrs. Welman. My dear mistress. Passed away in her sleep.'

'Aunt Laura? Dead?'

Elinor stared. She seemed unable to take it in.

Mrs. Bishop was weeping now with more abandon.

'To think of it,' she sobbed. 'After all these years! Eighteen years I've been here. But indeed it doesn't seem like it. . . .'

Elinor said slowly:

'So Aunt Laura died in her sleep—quite peacefully. . . . What a blessing for her!'

Mrs. Bishop wept.

'So *sudden*. The doctor saying he'd call again this morning and everything just as usual.'

Elinor said rather sharply:

'It wasn't exactly *sudden*. After all, she'd been ill for some time. I'm just so thankful she's been spared more suffering.'

Mrs. Bishop said tearfully that there was indeed that to be thankful for. She added:

'Who'll tell Mr. Roderick?'

Elinor said:

'I will.'

She threw on a dressing-gown and went along to his door and tapped. His voice answered, saying, 'Come in.'

She entered.

'Aunt Laura's dead, Roddy. She died in her sleep.'

Roddy, sitting up in bed, drew a deep sigh.

'Poor dear Aunt Laura! Thank God for it, I say. I couldn't have borne to see her go on lingering in the state she was yesterday.'

Elinor said mechanically:

'I didn't know you'd seen her?'

He nodded rather shamefacedly.

'The truth is, Elinor, I felt the most awful coward, because I'd funked it! I went along there yesterday evening. The nurse, the fat one, left the room for something—went down with a hot-water bottle, I think—and I slipped in. She didn't know I was there, of course. I just stood a bit and looked at her. Then, when I heard Mrs. Gamp stumping up the stairs again, I slipped away. But it was—pretty terrible!'

Elinor nodded.

'Yes, it was.'

Roddy said:

'She'd have hated it like hell—every minute of it!'

'I know.'

Roddy said:

'It's marvellous the way you and I always see alike over things.'

Elinor said in a low voice:

'Yes, it is.'

He said:

'We're both feeling the same thing at this minute: *just utter thankfulness that she's out of it all. . . .*'

II

Nurse O'Brien said:

'What is it, Nurse? Can't you find something?'

Nurse Hopkins, her face rather red, was hunting through the little attaché-case that she had laid down in the hall the preceding evening.

She grunted:

'Most annoying. How I came to do such a thing I can't imagine!'

'What is it?'

Nurse Hopkins replied not very intelligibly:

'It's Eliza Rykin—that sarcoma, you know. She's got to have double injections—night and morning—morphine. Gave her the last tablet in the old tube last night on my way here, and I could swear I had the new tube in here, too.'

'Look again. Those tubes are so small.'

Nurse Hopkins gave a final stir to the contents of the attaché-case.

44

'No, it's not here! I must have left it in my cupboard after all! Really, I did think I could trust my memory better than *that*. I could have sworn I took it out with me!'

'You didn't leave the case anywhere, did you, on the way here?'

'Of course not!' said Nurse Hopkins sharply.

'Oh, well, dear,' said Nurse O'Brien, 'it must be all *right?*'

'Oh, yes! The only place I've laid my case down was here in this hall, and nobody *here* would pinch anything! Just my memory, I suppose. But it vexes me, if you understand, Nurse. Besides, I shall have to go right home first to the other end of the village and back again.'

Nurse O'Brien said:

'Hope you won't have too tiring a day, dear, after last night. Poor old lady. I didn't think she would last long.'

'No, nor I. I daresay *Doctor* will be surprised!'

Nurse O'Brien said with a tinge of disapproval:

'He's always so *hopeful* about his cases.'

Nurse Hopkins, as she prepared to depart, said:

'Ah, he's young! He hasn't our experience.'

On which gloomy pronouncement she departed.

III

Dr. Lord raised himself up on his toes. His sandy eyebrows climbed right up his forehead till they nearly got merged in his hair.

He said in surprise:

'So she's conked out—eh?'

'Yes, Doctor.'

On Nurse O'Brien's tongue exact details were tingling to be uttered, but with stern discipline she waited.

Peter Lord said thoughtfully:

'Conked out?'

He stood for a moment thinking, then he said sharply:

'Get me some boiling water.'

Nurse O'Brien was surprised and mystified, but true to the spirit of hospital training, hers not to reason why. If a doctor had told her to go and get the skin of an alligator she would have murmured automatically, 'Yes, Doctor,' and glided obediently from the room to tackle the problem.

Roderick Welman said:

'Do you mean to say that my aunt died *intestate*—that she never made a will at *all*?'

Mr. Seddon polished his eyeglasses. He said:

'That seems to be the case.'

Roddy said:

'But how extraordinary!'

Mr. Seddon gave a deprecating cough.

'Not so extraordinary as you might imagine. It happens oftener than you would think. There's a kind of superstition about it. People *will* think they've got plenty of time. The mere fact of making a will seems to bring the possibility of death nearer to them. Very odd—but there it is!'

Roddy said:

'Didn't you ever—er—expostulate with her on the subject?'

Mr. Seddon replied dryly:

'Frequently.'

'And what did she say?'

Mr. Seddon sighed.

'The usual things. That there was plenty of time! That she didn't intend to die just yet! That she hadn't made up her mind definitely, exactly how she wished to dispose of her money!'

Elinor said:

'But surely, after her first stroke——?'

Mr. Seddon shook his head.

'Oh, no, it was worse then. She wouldn't hear the subject mentioned!'

Roddy said:

'Surely that's very odd?'

Mr. Seddon said again:

'Oh, no. Naturally, her illness made her much more nervous.'

Elinor said in a puzzled voice:

'But she wanted to die. . . .'

Polishing his eyeglasses, Mr. Seddon said:

'Ah, my dear Miss Elinor, the human mind is a very curious piece of mechanism. Mrs. Welman may have *thought* she wanted to die; but side by side with that feeling there ran the hope that she would recover absolutely. And because of that hope, I think she felt that to make a will would be unlucky. It isn't so much that she didn't mean to make one, as that she was eternally putting it off.'

'*You* know,' went on Mr. Seddon, suddenly addressing Roddy in an almost personal manner, 'how one puts off and avoids a thing that is distasteful—that you don't want to face?'

Roddy flushed. He muttered:

'Yes, I—I—yes, of course. I know what you mean.'

'Exactly,' said Mr. Seddon. 'Mrs. Welman always *meant* to make a will, but to-morrow was always a better day to make it than to-day! She kept telling herself that there was plenty of time.'

Elinor said slowly:

'So that's why she was so upset last night—and in such a panic that you should be sent for. . . .'

Mr. Seddon replied:

'Undoubtedly!'

Roddy said in a bewildered voice:

'But what happens now?'

'To Mrs. Welman's estate?' The lawyer coughed. 'Since Mrs. Welman died intestate, all her property goes to her next of kin—that is, to Miss Elinor Carlisle.'

Elinor said slowly:

'All to *me*?'

'The Crown takes a certain percentage,' Mr. Seddon explained.

He went into details.

He ended:

'There are no settlements or trusts. Mrs. Welman's money was hers absolutely to do with as she chose. It passes, therefore, straight to Miss Carlisle. Er—the death duties, I am afraid, will be somewhat heavy, but even after their payment, the fortune will still be a considerable one, and it is very well invested in sound gilt-edged securities.'

Elinor said:

'But Roderick——'

Mr. Seddon said with a little apologetic cough:

'Mr. Welman is only Mrs. Welman's *husband's* nephew. There is no blood relationship.'

'Quite,' said Roddy.

Elinor said slowly:

'Of course, it doesn't much matter which of us gets it, as

47

we're going to be married.'

But she did not look at Roddy.

It was Mr. Seddon's turn to say, 'Quite!'

He said it rather quickly.

V

'But it doesn't matter, does it?' Elinor said.

She spoke almost pleadingly.

Mr. Seddon had departed.

Roddy's face twitched nervously.

He said:

'You ought to have it. It's quite right you should. For heaven's sake, Elinor, don't get it into your head that I grudge it to you. *I* don't want the damned money!'

Elinor said, her voice slightly unsteady:

'We did agree, Roddy, in London that it wouldn't matter which of us it was, as—as we were going to be married . . .?'

He did not answer. She persisted:

'Don't you remember saying that, Roddy?'

He said:

'Yes.'

He looked down at his feet. His face was white and sullen, there was pain in the taut lines of his sensitive mouth.

Elinor said with a sudden gallant lift of the head:

'It doesn't matter—*if we're going to be married. . . . But are we, Roddy?*'

He said:

'Are we what?'

'Are we going to marry each other?'

'I understood that was the idea.'

His tone was indifferent, with a slight edge to it. He went on:

'Of course, Elinor, if you've other ideas now . . .'

Elinor cried out:

'Oh, Roddy, can't you be *honest*?'

He winced.

Then he said in a low, bewildered voice:

'I don't know what's happened to me. . . .'

Elinor said in a stifled voice:

'I do . . .'

He said quickly:

'Perhaps it's true, that. I don't after all, quite like the idea of living on my wife's money. . . .'

Elinor, her face white, said:

'It's not that. . . . It's something else. . . .' She paused, then she said, 'It's—Mary, isn't it?'

Roddy muttered unhappily:

'I suppose so. How did you know?'

Elinor said, her mouth twisting sideways in a crooked smile:

'It wasn't difficult. . . . Every time you look at her—it's there in your face for anyone to read. . . .'

Suddenly his composure broke.

'Oh, Elinor—I don't know what's the matter! I think I'm going mad! It happened when I saw her—that first day—in the wood . . . just her face—it's—it's turned everything upside-down. *You* can't understand that . . .'

Elinor said:

'Yes, I can. Go on.'

Roddy said helplessly:

'I didn't want to fall in love with her . . . I was quite happy with you. Oh, Elinor, what a cad I am, talking like this to you——'

Elinor said:

'Nonsense. Go on. Tell me. . . .'

He said brokenly:

'You're wonderful. . . . Talking to you helps frightfully. I'm so terribly fond of you, Elinor! You must believe that. This other thing is like an enchantment! It's upset everything: my conception of life—and my enjoyment of things—and—all the decent ordered reasonable things. . . .'

Elinor said gently:

'Love—isn't very reasonable. . . .'

Roddy said miserably:

'No. . . .'

Elinor said, and her voice trembled a little:

'Have you said anything to her?'

Roddy said:

'This morning—like a fool—I lost my head——'

Elinor said:

'Yes?'

Roddy said:

'Of course she—she shut me up at once! She was shocked. Because of Aunt Laura and—of *you*——'

Elinor drew the diamond ring off her finger. She said:

'You'd better take it back, Roddy.'

Taking it, he murmured without looking at her:

'Elinor, you've no idea what a beast I feel.'

Elinor said in her calm voice:

'Do you think she'll marry you?'

He shook his head.

'I've no idea. Not—not for a long time. I don't think she cares for me now; but she might come to care. . . .'

Elinor said:

'I think you're right. You must give her time. Not see her for a bit, and then—start afresh.'

'Darling Elinor! You're the best friend anyone ever had.' He took her hand suddenly and kissed it. 'You know, Elinor, I *do love* you—just as much as ever! Sometimes Mary seems just like a dream. I might wake up from it—and find she wasn't there. . . .'

Elinor said:

'If Mary wasn't there . . .'

Roddy said with sudden feeling:

'Sometimes I wish she wasn't. . . . You and I, Elinor, *belong*. We do belong, don't we?'

Slowly she bent her head.

She said:

'Oh, yes—we belong.'

She thought:

'*If Mary wasn't there . . .*'

CHAPTER FIVE

I

Nurse Hopkins said with emotion:

'It was a beautiful funeral!'

Nurse O'Brien responded:

'It was, indeed. And the flowers! Did you ever see such beautiful flowers? A harp of white lilies there was, and a cross of yellow roses. Beautiful!'

Nurse Hopkins sighed and helped herself to buttered tea-cake. The two nurses were sitting in the Blue Tit Café.

Nurse Hopkins went on:

'Miss Carlisle is a generous girl. She gave me a nice present, though she'd no call to do so.'

'She's a fine generous girl,' agreed Nurse O'Brien warmly. 'I do detest stinginess.'

Nurse Hopkins said:

'Well, it's a grand fortune she's inherited.'

Nurse O'Brien said, 'I wonder . . .' and stopped.

Nurse Hopkins said, 'Yes?' encouragingly.

' 'Twas strange the way the old lady made no will.'

'It was wicked,' Nurse Hopkins said sharply. 'People ought to be forced to make wills! It only leads to unpleasantness when they don't.'

'I'm wondering,' said Nurse O'Brien, 'if she *had* made a will, how she'd have left her money?'

Nurse Hopkins said firmly:

'I know *one* thing.'

'What's that?'

'She'd have left a sum of money to Mary—Mary Gerrard.'

'Yes, indeed, and that's true,' agreed the other. She added excitedly, 'Wasn't I after telling you that night of the state she was in, poor dear, and the doctor doing his best to calm her down. Miss Elinor was there holding her auntie's hand and swearing by God Almighty,' said Nurse O'Brien, her Irish imagination suddenly running away with her, 'that the lawyer should be sent for and everything done accordingly. "Mary! Mary!" the poor old lady said. "Is it Mary Gerrard you're meaning?" says Miss Elinor, and straightaway she swore that Mary should have her rights!'

Nurse Hopkins said rather doubtfully:

'Was it like that?'

Nurse O'Brien replied firmly:

'That was the way of it, and I'll tell you this, Nurse Hopkins: In my opinion, if Mrs. Welman had lived to make that will, it's likely there might have been surprises for all! Who knows she mightn't have left every penny she possessed to Mary Gerrard!'

Nurse Hopkins said dubiously:

'I don't think she'd do that. I don't hold with leaving your money away from your own flesh and blood.'

Nurse O'Brien said oracularly:

'There's flesh and blood and flesh and blood.'

Nurse Hopkins responded instantly:

'Now, what might you mean by *that*?'

Nurse O'Brien said with dignity:

'I'm not one to gossip! And I wouldn't be blackening anyone's name that's dead.'

Nurse Hopkins nodded her head slowly and said:

'That's right. I agree with you. Least said soonest mended.' She filled up the teapot.

Nurse O'Brien said:

'By the way, now, did you find that tube of morphine all right when you got home?'

Nurse Hopkins frowned. She said:

'No. It beats me to know what can have become of it, but I think it may have been this way: I *might* have set it down on the edge of the mantelpiece as I often do while I lock the cupboard, and it *might* have rolled and fallen into the waste-paper basket that was all full of rubbish and that was emptied out into the dustbin just as I left the house.' She paused. 'It *must* be that way, for I don't see what else could have become of it.'

'I see,' said Nurse O'Brien. 'Well, dear, that must have been it. It's not as though you'd left your case about anywhere else —only just in the hall at Hunterbury—so it seems to me that what you suggested just now must be so. It's gone into the rubbish bin.'

'That's right,' said Nurse Hopkins eagerly. 'It couldn't be any other way, could it?'

She helped herself to a pink sugar cake. She said, 'It's not as though . . .' and stopped.

The other agreed quickly—perhaps a little too quickly.

'I'd not be worrying about it any more if I was you,' she said comfortably.

Nurse Hopkins said:

'I'm *not* worrying. . . .'

II

Young and severe in her black dress, Elinor sat in front of Mrs. Welman's massive writing-table in the library. Various papers were spread out in front of her. She had finished interviewing the servants and Mrs. Bishop. Now it was Mary Gerrard who entered the room and hesitated a minute by the doorway.

'You wanted to see me, Miss Elinor?' she said.

Elinor looked up.

'Oh, yes, Mary. Come here and sit down, will you?'

Mary came and sat in the chair Elinor indicated. It was turned a little towards the window, and the light from it fell on her face, showing the dazzling purity of the skin and bringing out the pale gold of the girl's hair.

Elinor held one hand shielding her face a little. Between the fingers she could watch the other girl's face.

She thought:

'Is it possible to hate anyone so much and not show it?'

Aloud she said in a pleasant, businesslike voice:

'I think you know, Mary, that my aunt always took a great interest in you and would have been concerned about your future.'

Mary murmured in her soft voice:

'Mrs. Welman was very good to me always.'

Elinor went on, her voice cold and detached:

'My aunt, if she had had time to make a will, would have wished, I know, to leave several legacies. Since she died without making a will, the responsibility of carrying out her wishes rests on me. I have consulted with Mr. Seddon, and by his advice we have drawn up a schedule of sums for the servants according to their length of service, etc.' She paused. 'You, of course, don't come quite into that class.'

She half-hoped, perhaps, that those words might hold a sting, but the face she was looking at showed no change. Mary accepted the words at their face value and listened to what more was to come.

Elinor said:

'Though it was difficult for my aunt to speak coherently, she was able to make her meaning understood that last evening. She definitely wanted to make some provision for your future.'

Mary said quietly:

'That was very good of her.'

Elinor said brusquely:

'As soon as probate is granted, I am arranging that two thousand pounds should be made over to you—that sum to be yours to do with absolutely as you please.'

Mary's colour rose.

'Two thousand pounds? Oh, Miss Elinor, that *is* good of you! I don't know what to say.'

Elinor said sharply:

'It isn't particularly good of me, and please don't say anything.'

Mary flushed.

'You don't know what a difference it will make to me,' she murmured.

Elinor said:

'I'm glad.'

She hesitated. She looked away from Mary to the other side of the room. She said with a slight effort:

'I wonder—have you any plans?'

Mary said quickly:

'Oh, yes. I shall train for something. Massage, perhaps. That's what Nurse Hopkins advises.'

Elinor said:

'That sounds a very good idea. I will try and arrange with Mr. Seddon that some money shall be advanced to you as soon as possible—at once, if that is feasible.'

'You're very, *very* good, Miss Elinor,' said Mary gratefully.

Elinor said curtly:

'It was Aunt Laura's wish.' She hesitated, then said, 'Well, that's all, I think.'

This time the definite dismissal in the words pierced Mary's sensitive skin. She got up, said quietly, 'Thank you very much, Miss Elinor,' and left the room.

Elinor sat quite still, staring ahead of her. Her face was quite impassive. There was no clue in it as to what was going on in her mind. But she sat there, motionless, for a long time.

ɑ ɔ ʮ

III

Elinor went at last in search of Roddy. She found him in the morning-room. He was standing staring out of the window. He turned sharply as Elinor came in.

She said:

'I've got through it all! Five hundred for Mrs. Bishop— she's been here such years. A hundred for the cook and fifty each for Milly and Olive. Five pounds each to the others. Twenty-five for Stephens, the head gardener; and there's old Gerrard, of course, at the Lodge. I haven't done anything about him yet. It's awkward. He'll have to be pensioned off, I suppose?'

She paused and then went on rather hurriedly:

'I'm settling two thousand on Mary Gerrard. Do you

think that's what Aunt Laura would have wished? It seemed to me about the right sum.'

Roddy said without looking at her:

'Yes, exactly right. You've always got excellent judgment, Elinor.'

He turned to look out of the window again.

Elinor held her breath for a minute, then she began to speak with nervous haste, the words tumbling out incoherently:

'There's something more: I want to—it's only right—I mean, *you*'ve got to have your proper share, Roddy.'

As he wheeled round, anger on his face, she hurried on:

'No, *listen*, Roddy. This is just bare justice! The money that was your uncle's—that he left to his wife—naturally he always assumed it would come to you. Aunt Laura meant it to, too. I know she did, from lots of things she said. If *I* have *her* money, *you* should have the amount that was *his*—it's only right. I—I can't bear to feel that I've robbed you—just because Aunt Laura funked making a will. You must—you *must* see sense about this!'

Roderick's long, sensitive face had gone dead white.

He said:

'My God, Elinor, do you want to make me feel an utter cad? Do you think for one moment I could—could take this money from you?'

'I'm not *giving* it to you. It's just—fair.'

Roddy cried out:

'I don't want your money!'

'It isn't mine!'

'It's yours by law—and that's all that matters! For God's sake, don't let's be anything but strictly businesslike! I won't take a penny from you. You're not going to do the Lady Bountiful to me!'

Elinor cried out:

'Roddy!'

He made a quick gesture.

'Oh, my dear, I'm sorry. I don't know what I'm saying. I feel so bewildered—so utterly lost. . . .'

Elinor said gently:

'Poor Roddy. . . .'

He had turned away again and was playing with the blind tassel of the window. He said in a different tone, a detached one:

'Do you know what—Mary Gerrard proposes doing?'

'She's going to train as a masseuse, so she says.'

He said, 'I see.'

There was a silence. Elinor drew herself up; she flung back her head. Her voice when she spoke was suddenly compelling. She said:

'Roddy, I want you to listen to me carefully!'

He turned to her, slightly surprised.

'Of course, Elinor.'

'I want you, if you will, to follow my advice.'

'And what is your advice?'

Elinor said calmly:

'You are not particularly tied? You can always get a holiday, can't you?'

'Oh, yes.'

'Then do—just that. Go abroad somewhere for—say, three months. Go by yourself. Make new friends and see new places. Let's speak quite frankly. At this moment you think you're in love with Mary Gerrard. Perhaps you are. But it isn't a moment for approaching her—you know that only too well. Our engagement is definitely broken off. Go abroad, then, as a free man, and at the end of the three months, as a free man, make up your mind. You'll know then whether you—really love Mary or whether it was only a temporary infatuation. And if you are quite sure you *do* love her—well, then, come back and go to her and tell her so, and that you're quite sure about it, and perhaps then she'll listen.'

Roddy came to her. He caught her hand in his.

'Elinor, you're wonderful! So clear-headed! So marvellously impersonal! There's no trace of pettiness or meanness about you. I admire you more than I can ever say. I'll do exactly what you suggest. Go away, cut free from everything —and find out whether I've got the genuine disease or if I've just been making the most ghastly fool of myself. Oh, Elinor, my dear, you don't know how truly fond I am of you. I do realise you were always a thousand times too good for me. Bless you, dear, for all your goodness.'

Quickly, impulsively, he kissed her cheek and went out of the room.

It was as well, perhaps, that he did not look back and see her face.

It was a couple of days later that Mary acquainted Nurse Hopkins with her improved prospects.

That practical woman was warmly congratulatory.

'That's a great piece of luck for you, Mary,' she said. 'The old lady may have meant well by you, but unless a thing's down in black and white, intentions don't go for much! You might easily have got nothing at all.'

'Miss Elinor said that the night Mrs. Welman died she told her to do something for me.'

Nurse Hopkins snorted.

'Maybe she did. But there's many would have forgotten conveniently afterwards. Relations are like that. I've seen a few things, *I* can tell you! People dying and saying they know they can leave it to their dear son or their dear daughter to carry out their wishes. Nine times out of ten, dear son and dear daughter find some very good reason to do nothing of the kind. Human nature's human nature, and nobody likes parting with money if they're not legally compelled to! I tell you, Mary, my girl, you've been lucky. Miss Carlisle's straighter than most.'

Mary said slowly:

'And yet—somehow—I feel she doesn't like me.'

'With good reason, I should say,' said Nurse Hopkins bluntly. 'Now, don't look so innocent, Mary! Mr. Roderick's been making sheep's eyes at you for some time now.'

Mary went red.

Nurse Hopkins went on:

'He's got it badly, in my opinion. Fell for you all of a sudden. What about you, my girl? Got any feelings for him?'

Mary said hesitatingly:

'I—I don't know. I don't think so. But of course, he's very nice.'

'H'm,' said Nurse Hopkins. 'He wouldn't be *my* fancy! One of those men who are finicky and a bundle of nerves. Fussy about their food, too, as likely as not. Men aren't much at the best of times. Don't be in too much of a hurry, Mary, my dear. With your looks you can afford to pick and choose. Nurse O'Brien passed the remark to me the other day that you ought to go on the films. They like blondes, I've always heard.'

Mary said, with a slight frown creasing her forehead:

'Nurse, what do you think I ought to do about Father? He thinks I ought to give some of this money to him.'

'Don't you do anything of the kind,' said Nurse Hopkins wrathfully. 'Mrs. Welman never meant that money for him. It's my opinion he'd have lost his job years ago if it hadn't been for you. A lazier man never stepped!'

Mary said:

'It seems funny when she'd all that money that she never made a will to say how it was to go.'

Nurse Hopkins shook her head.

'People are like that. You'd be surprised. Always putting it off.'

Mary said:

'It seems downright silly to me.'

Nurse Hopkins said with a faint twinkle:

'Made a will yourself, Mary?'

Mary stared at her.

'Oh, no.'

'And yet you're over twenty-one.'

'But I—I haven't got anything to leave—at least I suppose I have now.'

Nurse Hopkins said sharply:

'Of course you have. And a nice tidy little sum, too.'

Mary said:

'Oh, well, there's no hurry . . .'

'There you go,' said Nurse Hopkins dryly. 'Just like everyone else. Because you're a healthy young girl isn't a reason why you shouldn't be smashed up in a charabanc or a bus, or run over in the street any minute.'

Mary laughed. She said:

'I don't even know how to make a will.'

'Easy enough. You can get a form at the post office. Let's go and get one right away.'

In Nurse Hopkins' cottage, the form was spread out and the important matter discussed. Nurse Hopkins was enjoying herself thoroughly. A will, as she said, was next best to a death, in her opinion.

Mary said:

'Who'd get the money if I didn't make a will?'

Nurse Hopkins said rather doubtfully:

'Your father, I suppose.'

Mary said sharply:

'He shan't have it. I'd rather leave it to my auntie in New Zealand.'

Nurse Hopkins said cheerfully:

'It wouldn't be much use leaving it to your father, anyway—*he's* not long for this world, I should say.'

Mary had heard Nurse Hopkins make this kind of pronouncement too often to be impressed by it.

'I can't remember my auntie's address. We've not heard from her for years.'

'I don't suppose that matters,' said Nurse Hopkins. 'You know her Christian name?'

'Mary. Mary Riley.'

'That's all right. Put down you leave everything to Mary Riley, sister of the late Eliza Gerrard of Hunterbury, Maidensford.'

Mary bent over the form, writing. As she came to the end she shivered suddenly. A shadow had come between her and the sun. She looked up to see Elinor Carlisle standing outside the window looking in. Elinor said:

'What are you doing so busily?'

Nurse Hopkins said with a laugh:

'She's making her will, that's what she's doing.'

'Making her will?' Suddenly Elinor laughed—a strange laugh—almost hysterical.

She said:

'So you're making your will, Mary. *That's funny. That's very funny.* . . .'

Still laughing, she turned away and walked rapidly along the street.

Nurse Hopkins stared.

'Did you ever? What's come to her?'

v

Elinor had not taken more than half a dozen steps—she was still laughing—when a hand fell on her arm from behind. She stopped abruptly and turned.

Dr. Lord looked straight at her, his brow creased into a frown.

He said peremptorily:

'What were you laughing at?'

Elinor said:

'Really—I don't know.'

Peter Lord said:

'That's rather a silly answer!'

Elinor flushed. She said:

'I think I must be nervous—or something. I looked in at the District Nurse's cottage and—and Mary Gerrard was writing out her will. It made me laugh; I don't know why!'

Lord said abruptly:

'*Don't you?*'

Elinor said:

'It was silly of me—I tell you—I'm nervous.'

Peter Lord said:

'I'll write you out a tonic.'

Elinor said incisively:

'How useful!'

He grinned disarmingly.

'Quite useless, I agree. But it's the only thing one can do when people won't tell one what is the matter with them!'

Elinor said:

'There's nothing the matter with me.'

Peter Lord said calmly:

'There's quite a lot the matter with you.'

Elinor said:

'I've had a certain amount of nervous strain, I suppose . . .'

He said:

'I expect you've had quite a lot. But that's not what I'm talking about.' He paused. 'Are you—are you staying down here much longer?'

'I'm leaving to-morrow.'

'You won't—live down here?'

Elinor shook her head.

'No—never. I think—I think—I shall sell the place if I can get a good offer.'

Dr. Lord said rather flatly:

'I see . . .'

Elinor said:

'I must be getting home now.'

She held out her hand firmly. Peter Lord took it. He held it. He said very earnestly:

'Miss Carlisle, will you please tell me what was in your mind when you laughed just now?'

She wrenched her hand away quickly.

'What should there be in my mind?'

'That's what I'd like to know.'

His face was grave and a little unhappy.

Elinor said impatiently:

'It just struck me as funny, that was all!'

'That Mary Gerrard was making a will? Why? Making a will is a perfectly sensible procedure. Saves a lot of trouble. Sometimes, of course, it *makes* trouble!'

Elinor said impatiently:

'Of course—everyone should make a will. I didn't mean that.'

Dr. Lord said:

'Mrs. Welman ought to have made a will.'

Elinor said with feeling:

'Yes, indeed.'

The colour rose in her face.

Dr. Lord said unexpectedly:

'What about you?'

'*Me?*'

'Yes, you said just now everyone should make a will! Have *you*?'

Elinor stared at him for a minute, then she laughed.

'How extraordinary!' she said. 'No, I haven't. I hadn't thought of it! I'm just like Aunt Laura. Do you know. Dr. Lord, I shall go home and write to Mr. Seddon about it at once.'

Peter Lord said:

'Very sensible.'

VI

In the library Elinor had just finished a letter:

> '*Dear Mr. Seddon,—Will you draft a will for me to sign? Quite a simple one. I want to leave everything to Roderick Welman absolutely*,
>
> > '*Yours sincerely,*
> >
> > > '*Elinor Carlisle*.'

She glanced at the clock. The post would be going in a few minutes.

She opened the drawer of the desk, then remembered she had used the last stamp that morning.

There were some in her bedroom, though, she was almost sure.

She went upstairs. When she re-entered the library with the stamp in her hand, Roddy was standing by the window.

He said:

'So we leave here to-morrow. Good old Hunterbury. We've had some good times here.'

Elinor said:

'Do you mind its being sold?'

'Oh, no, no! I quite see it's the best thing to be done.'

There was a silence. Elinor picked up her letter, glanced through it to see if it was all right. Then she sealed and stamped it.

CHAPTER SIX

I

Letter from Nurse O'Brien to Nurse Hopkins, July 14th:

'Laborough Court

'DEAR HOPKINS,—Have been meaning to write to you for some days now. This is a lovely house and the pictures, I believe, quite famous. But I can't say it's as comfortable as Hunterbury was, if you know what I mean. Being in the dead country it's difficult to get maids, and the girls they have got are a raw lot, and some of them not too obliging, and though I'm sure I'm never one to give trouble, meals sent up on a tray should at least be hot, and no facilities for boiling a kettle, and the tea *not* always made with boiling water! Still, all that's neither here nor there. The patient's a nice quiet gentleman—double pneumonia, but the crisis is past and doctor says going on well.

'What I've got to tell you that will really interest you is the very queerest coincidence you ever knew. In the drawing-room, on the grand piano, there's a photograph in a big silver frame, and would you believe it, it's the same photograph that I told you about—the one signed *Lewis* that old Mrs. Welman asked for. Well, of course, I *was* intrigued—and who wouldn't be? And I asked the butler who it was, which he answered at once saying it was Lady Rattery's brother—Sir Lewis Rycroft. He lived, it seems, not far from here and he was killed in the War. Very sad, wasn't it? I asked casual like was he married, and the butler said yes, but that Lady Rycroft went into a lunatic asylum, poor thing, soon after the marriage. She was still alive, he said. Now, isn't that interesting? And we were quite wrong, you see, in all our ideas. They must have been very fond of each other, he and Mrs. W., and unable to marry because of the wife being in an asylum. Just like the pictures, isn't it? And her remembering all those years and looking at his photograph just before she died. He was killed in 1917, the butler said. Quite a romance, that's what *I* feel.

'Have you seen that new picture with Myrna Loy? I saw it was coming to Maidensford this week. No cinema anywhere near here! Oh, it's awful to be buried in the country. No wonder they can't get decent maids!

'Well, good-bye for the present, dear, write and tell me *all* the news.

'Yours sincerely,
'EILEEN O'BRIEN.'

Letter from Nurse Hopkins to Nurse O'Brien, July 14th:

'*Rose Cottage*

'DEAR O'BRIEN,—Everything goes on here much as usual. Hunterbury is deserted—all the servants gone and a board up: For Sale. I saw Mrs. Bishop the other day, she is staying with her sister who lives about a mile away. She was very upset, as you can imagine, at the place being sold. It seems she made sure Miss Carlisle would marry Mr. Welman and live there. Mrs. B. says that the engagement is off! Miss Carlisle went away to London soon after you left. She was *very* peculiar in her manner once or twice. I really didn't know what to make of her! Mary Gerrard has gone to London and is starting to train for a masseuse. Very sensible of her, I think. Miss Carlisle's going to settle two thousand pounds on her, which I call very handsome and more than what many would do.

'By the way, it's funny how things come about. Do you remember telling me something about a photograph signed *Lewis* that Mrs. Welman showed you? I was having a chat the other day with Mrs. Slattery (she was housekeeper to old Dr. Ransome who had the practice before Dr. Lord), and of course she's lived here all her life and knows a lot about the gentry round about. I just brought the subject up in a casual manner, speaking of Christian names and saying that the name of Lewis was uncommon and amongst others she mentioned Sir Lewis Rycroft over at Forbes Park. He served in the War in the 17th Lancers and was killed towards the end of the War. So I said *he was a great-friend of Mrs. Welman's at Hunterbury, wasn't he?* And at once she gave me a *look* and said, *Yes, very* close friends they'd been, and *some said more than friends*, but that she herself wasn't one to *talk*—and why shouldn't they be friends? So I said but surely Mrs. Welman was a *widow* at the time, and she said Oh yes, *she* was a widow. So, dear, I saw *at once* she meant something by *that*, so I said it was odd then, that they'd never married, and she said at once, "They couldn't marry. He'd got a *wife* in a *lunatic asylum!*" So now, you see, we know *all* about it! Curious the way things come about, isn't it? Considering the easy way you get divorces nowadays, it does seem a shame that insanity shouldn't have been a ground for it then.

'Do you remember a good-looking young chap, Ted Bigland, who used to hang around after Mary Gerrard a lot? He's been at me for her address in London, but I haven't given it to him. In my opinion, Mary's a cut above Ted Bigland. I don't know if you realised it, dear, but Mr. R—— W—— was very taken with her. A pity, because it's made trouble. Mark my words, that's the reason for the engagement between him and Miss Carlisle being off. And, if you ask me, it's hit *her badly*. I don't know what she saw in *him*, I'm sure—he wouldn't have been my cup of tea, but I hear from a reliable source that she's always been *madly* in love with him. It does seem a mix-up, doesn't it? And she's got all that money, too. I believe he was always led to expect his aunt would leave him something substantial.

'Old Gerrard at the Lodge is failing rapidly—has had several nasty dizzy spells. He's just as rude and cross-grained as ever. He actually said the other day that Mary wasn't his daughter. "Well," I said, "I'd be *ashamed* to say a thing like that about your wife if I were you." He just looked at me and said, "You're nothing but a fool. You don't understand." Polite, wasn't it? I took him up pretty sharply, I can tell you. His wife was lady's maid to Mrs. Welman before her marriage, I believe.

'I saw *The Good Earth* last week. It was lovely! Women have to put up with a lot in China, it seems.

'Yours ever,
'JESSIE HOPKINS.'

Post-card from Nurse Hopkins to Nurse O'Brien:

'Fancy our letters just crossing! Isn't this weather awful?'

Post-card from Nurse O'Brien to Nurse Hopkins:

'Got your letter this morning. What a *coincidence*!'

Letter from Roderick Welman to Elinor Carlisle, July 15th:

'DEAR ELINOR,—Just got your letter. No, really, I have *no* feelings about Hunterbury being sold. Nice of you to consult me. I think you're doing the wisest thing if you don't fancy living there, which you obviously don't. You may have some difficulty in getting rid of it, though. It's a biggish place for present-day needs, though, of course, it's been modernised and is up to date, with good servants' quarters, and gas and electric light and all that. Anyway, I hope you'll have luck!

'The heat here is glorious. I spend hours in the sea. Rather a funny crowd of people, but I don't mix much. You told me once that I wasn't a good mixer. I'm afraid it's true. I find most of the human race extraordinarily repulsive. They probably reciprocate this feeling.

'I have long felt that you are one of the only really satisfactory representatives of humanity. Am thinking of wandering on to the Dalmatian coast in a week or two. Address c/o Thomas Cook, Dubrovnik, from the 22nd onwards. If there's anything I can do, let me know.

'Yours, with admiration and gratitude,
'RODDY.'

Letter from Mr. Seddon of Messrs. Seddon, Blatherwick & Seddon to Miss Elinor Carlisle, July 20th:

'104 *Bloomsbury Square*
'DEAR MISS CARLISLE,—I certainly think you should

accept Major Somervell's offer of twelve thousand five hundred (£12,500) for Hunterbury. Large properties are extremely difficult to sell at the moment, and the price offered seems to be most advantageous. The offer depends, however, on immediate possession, and I know Major Somervell has been seeing other properties in the neighbourhood, so I would advise immediate acceptance.

'Major Somervell is willing, I understand, to take the place furnished for three months, by which time the legal formalities should be accomplished and the sale can go through.

'As regards the lodge-keeper, Gerrard, and the question of pensioning him off, I hear from Dr. Lord that the old man is seriously ill and not expected to live.

'Probate has not yet been granted, but I have advanced one hundred pounds to Miss Mary Gerrard pending the settlement.

'Yours sincerely,
'EDMUND SEDDON.'

Letter from Dr. Lord to Miss Elinor Carlisle, July 24th:

'DEAR MISS CARLISLE,—Old Gerrard passed away to-day. Is there anything I can do for you in any way? I hear you have sold the house to our new M.P., Major Somervell.
'Yours sincerely,
'PETER LORD.'

Letter from Elinor Carlisle to Mary Gerrard, July 25th:

'DEAR MARY,—I am so sorry to hear of your father's death.

'I have had an offer for Hunterbury—from a Major Somervell. He is anxious to get in as soon as possible. I am going down there to go through my aunt's papers and clear up generally. Would it be possible for you to get your father's things moved out of the Lodge as quickly as possible? I hope you are doing well and not finding your massage training too strenuous.
'Yours very sincerely,
'ELINOR CARLISLE.'

Letter from Mary Gerrard to Nurse Hopkins, July 25th:

'DEAR NURSE HOPKINS,—Thank you so much for writing to me about Father. I'm glad he didn't suffer. Miss Elinor writes me that the house is sold and that she would like the Lodge cleared out as soon as possible. Could you put me up if I came down to-morrow for the funeral? Don't bother to answer if that's all right.

'Yours affectionately,

'MARY GERRARD.'

CHAPTER SEVEN

I

Elinor Carlisle came out of the King's Arms on the morning of Thursday, July 27th, and stood for a minute or two looking up and down the main street of Maidensford.

Suddenly, with an exclamation of pleasure, she crossed the road.

There was no mistaking that large dignified presence, that serene gait as of a galleon in full sail.

'Mrs. Bishop!'

'Why, Miss Elinor! This *is* a surprise! I'd no notion you were in these parts! If I'd known you were coming to Hunterbury I'd have been there myself! Who's doing for you there? Have you brought someone down from London?'

Elinor shook her head.

'I'm not staying at the house. I am staying at the King's Arms.'

Mrs. Bishop looked across the road and sniffed dubiously.

'It is *possible* to stay there, I've heard,' she allowed. 'It's clean, I know. And the cooking, they say, is fair, but it's hardly what *you're* accustomed to, Miss Elinor.'

Elinor said, smiling:

'I'm really quite comfortable. It's only for a day or two. I have to sort out things at the house. All my aunt's personal things; and then there are a few pieces of furniture I should like to have in London.'

'The house is really sold, then?'

'Yes. To a Major Somervell. Our new Member. Sir George Kerr died, you know, and there's been a bye-election.'

'Returned unopposed,' said Mrs. Bishop grandly. 'We've

67

never had anyone but a Conservative for Maidensford.'

Elinor said:

'I'm glad someone has bought the house who really wants to live in it. I should have been sorry if it had been turned into a hotel or built upon.'

Mrs. Bishop shut her eyes and shivered all over her plump aristocratic person.

'Yes, indeed, that would have been dreadful—quite dreadful. It's bad enough as it is to think of Hunterbury passing into the hands of strangers.'

Elinor said:

'Yes, but, you see, it would have been a very large house for me to live in—alone.'

Mrs. Bishop sniffed.

Elinor said quickly:

'I meant to ask you: Is there any especial piece of furniture that you might care to have? I should be very glad for you to have it, if so.'

Mrs. Bishop beamed. She said graciously:

'Well, Miss Elinor, that is very thoughtful of you—very kind, I'm sure. If it's not taking a liberty . . .'

She paused and Elinor said:

'Oh, no.'

'I have always had a great admiration for the secretaire in the drawing-room. Such a *handsome* piece.'

Elinor remembered it, a somewhat flamboyant piece of in-laid marqueterie. She said quickly:

'Of course you shall have it, Mrs. Bishop. Anything else?'

'No, indeed, Miss Elinor. You have already been extremely generous.'

Elinor said:

'There are some chairs in the same style as the secretaire. Would you care for those?'

Mrs. Bishop accepted the chairs with becoming thanks. She explained:

'I am staying at the moment with my sister. Is there anything I can do for you up at the house, Miss Elinor? I could come up there with you, if you like.'

'No, thank you.'

Elinor spoke quickly, rather abruptly.

Mrs. Bishop said:

'It would be no trouble, I assure you—a pleasure. Such a

melancholy task going through all dear Mrs. Welman's things.'

Elinor said:

'Thank you, Mrs. Bishop, but I would rather tackle it alone. One can do some things better alone——'

Mrs. Bishop said stiffly:

'As you please, of course.'

She went on:

'That daughter of Gerrard's is down here. The funeral was yesterday. She's staying with Nurse Hopkins. I did hear *they* were going up to the Lodge this morning.'

Elinor nodded. She said:

'Yes, I asked Mary to come down and see to that. Major Somervell wants to get in as soon as possible.'

'I see.'

Elinor said:

'Well, I must be getting on now. So glad to have seen you, Mrs. Bishop. I'll remember about the secretaire and the chairs.'

She shook hands and passed on.

She went into the baker's and bought a loaf of bread. Then she went into the dairy and bought half a pound of butter and some milk.

Finally she went into the grocer's.

'I want some paste for sandwiches, please.'

'Certainly, Miss Carlisle.' Mr. Abbott himself bustled forward, elbowing aside his junior apprentice.

'What would you like? Salmon and shrimp? Turkey and tongue? Salmon and sardine? Ham and tongue?'

He whipped down pot after pot and arrayed them on the counter.

Elinor said with a faint smile:

'In spite of their names, I always think they taste much alike.'

Mr. Abbott agreed instantly.

'Well, perhaps they do, in a way. Yes, in a way. But, of course, they're very tasty—very tasty.'

Elinor said:

'One used to be rather afraid of eating fish pastes. There have been cases of ptomaine poisoning from them, haven't there?'

Mr. Abbott put on a horrified expression.

'I can assure you this is an excellent brand—*most* reliable —we never have any complaints.'

Elinor said:

'I'll have one of salmon and anchovy and one of salmon and shrimp. Thank you.'

II

Elinor Carlisle entered the grounds of Hunterbury by the back gate.

It was a hot, clear summer's day. There were sweetpeas in flower. Elinor passed close by a row of them. The under-gardener, Horlick, who was remaining on to keep the place in order, greeted her respectfully.

'Good-morning, miss. I got your letter. You'll find the side door open, miss. I've unfastened the shutters and opened most of the windows.'

Elinor said:

'Thank you, Horlick.'

As she moved on, the young man said nervously, his Adam's apple jerking up and down in spasmodic fashion:

'Excuse me, miss——'

Elinor turned back. 'Yes?'

'Is it true that the house is sold? I mean, is it really settled?'

'Oh, yes!'

Horlick said nervously:

'I was wondering, miss, if you would say a word for me—to Major Somervell, I mean. He'll be wanting gardeners. Maybe he'll think I'm too young for head gardener, but I've worked under Mr. Stephens for four years now, and I reckon I know a tidyish bit, and I've kept things going fairly well since I've been here, single-handed.'

Elinor said quickly:

'Of course I will do all I can for you, Horlick. As a matter of fact, I intended to mention you to Major Somervell and tell him what a good gardener you are.'

Horlick's face grew dusky red.

'Thank you, miss. That's very kind of you. You can understand it's been a bit of a blow, like—Mrs. Welman dying, and then the place being sold off so quick—and I—well, the fact of the matter is I was going to get married this autumn, only one's got to be sure . . .'

He stopped.

Elinor said kindly:

'I hope Major Somervell will take you on. You can rely on me to do all I can.'

Horlick said again:

'Thank you, miss. We all hoped, you see, as how the place would be kept on by the family. Thank you, miss.'

Elinor walked on.

Suddenly, rushing over her like the stream from a broken dam, a wave of anger, of wild resentment, swept over her.

'We all hoped the place would be kept on by the family. . . .'

She and Roddy could have lived here! *She and Roddy.* . . . Roddy would have wanted that. It was what she herself would have wanted. They had always loved Hunterbury, both of them. Dear Hunterbury. . . . In the years before her parents had died, when they had been in India, she had come here for holidays. She had played in the woods, rambled by the stream, picked sweetpeas in great flowering armloads, eaten fat green gooseberries and dark red luscious raspberries. Later, there had been apples. There had been places, secret lairs, where she had curled up with a book and read for hours.

She had loved Hunterbury. Always, at the back of her mind, she had felt sure of living there permanently some day. Aunt Laura had fostered that idea. Little words and phrases:

'Some day, Elinor, you may like to cut down those yews. They are a little gloomy, perhaps!'

'One might have a water garden here. Some day, perhaps, *you* will.'

And Roddy? Roddy, too, had looked forward to Hunterbury being his home. It had lain, perhaps, behind his feeling for her, Elinor. He had felt, subconsciously, that it was fitting and right that they two should be together at Hunterbury.

And they *would* have been together there. They would have been together *here—now*—not packing up the house for selling, but redecorating it, planning new beauties in house and garden, walking side by side in gentle proprietary pleasure, happy—yes, *happy* together—but for the fatal accident of a girl's wild-rose beauty . . .

What did Roddy know of Mary Gerrard? Nothing—less than nothing! What did he care for her—for the real Mary? She had, quite possibly, admirable qualities, but did Roddy know anything about them? It was the old story—Nature's hoary old joke!

Hadn't Roddy himself said it was an 'enchantment'?

Didn't Roddy himself—*really*—want to be free of it?

If Mary Gerrard were to—die, for instance, wouldn't Roddy some day acknowledge: 'It was all for the best. I see that now. We had nothing in common. . . .'

He would add, perhaps, with gentle melancholy:

'She was a lovely creature. . . .'

Let her be that to him—yes—an exquisite memory—a thing of beauty and a joy for ever. . . .

If anything were to happen to Mary Gerrard, Roddy would come back to her—Elinor. . . . She was quite sure of that!

If anything were to happen to Mary Gerrard . . .

Elinor turned the handle of the side door. She passed from the warm sunlight into the shadow of the house. She shivered.

It felt cold in here, dark, sinister. . . . It was as though Something was there, waiting for her, in the house. . . .

She walked along the hall and pushed the baize door that led into the butler's pantry.

It smelt slightly musty. She pushed up the window, opening it wide.

She laid down her parcels—the butter, the loaf, the little glass bottle of milk. She thought:

'Stupid! I meant to get coffee.'

She looked in the canisters on a shelf. There was a little tea in one of them, but no coffee.

She thought: 'Oh, well, it doesn't matter.'

She unwrapped the two glass jars of fish paste.

She stood staring at them for a minute. Then she left the pantry and went upstairs. She went straight to Mrs. Welman's room. She began on the big tallboy, opening drawers, sorting, arranging, folding clothes in little piles. . . .

III

In the Lodge Mary Gerrard was looking round rather helplessly.

She hadn't realised, somehow, how cramped it all was.

Her past life rushed back over her in a flood. Mum making clothes for her dolls. Dad always cross and surly. Disliking her. Yes, disliking her. . . .

She said suddenly to Nurse Hopkins:

'Dad didn't say anything—send me any message before he died, did he?'

Nurse Hopkins said cheerfully and callously:

'Oh, dear me, no. He was unconscious for an hour before he passed away.'

Mary said slowly:

'I feel perhaps I ought to have come down and looked after him. After all, he *was* my father.'

Nurse Hopkins said with a trace of embarrassment:

'Now, just you listen to me, Mary: whether he was your father or not doesn't enter into it. Children don't care much about their parents in these days, from what I can see, and a good many parents don't care for their children, either. Miss Lambert, at the secondary school, says that's as it should be. According to her, family life is all wrong, and children should be brought up by the state. That's as may be—just a glorified orphanage, it sounds to me—but, anyway, it's a waste of breath to go back over the past and sentimentalise. We've got to get on with living—that's our job and not too easy, either, sometimes!'

Mary said slowly:

'I expect you're right. But I feel perhaps it was my fault we didn't get *on* better.'

Nurse Hopkins said robustly:

'Nonsense.'

The word exploded like a bomb.

It quelled Mary. Nurse Hopkins turned to more practical matters.

'What are you going to do with the furniture? Store it? Or sell it?'

Mary said doubtfully:

'I don't know. What do you think?'

Running a practical eye over it, Nurse Hopkins said:

'Some of it's quite good and solid. You might store it and furnish a little flat of your own in London some day. Get rid of the rubbish. The chairs are good—so's the table. And that's a nice bureau—it's the kind that's out of fashion, but it's solid mahogany, and they say Victorian stuff will come in again one day. I'd get rid of that great wardrobe, if I were you. Too big to fit in anywhere. Takes up half the bedroom as it is.'

They made a list between them of pieces to be kept or let go.

Mary said:

'The lawyer's been very kind—Mr. Seddon, I mean. He advanced me some money, so that I could get started with my training fees and other expenses. It will be a month or so before the money can be definitely made over to me, so he said.'

Nurse Hopkins said:

'How do you like your work?'

'I think I shall like it very much. It's rather strenuous at first. I come home tired to death.'

Nurse Hopkins said grimly:

'I thought I was going to die when I was a probationer at St. Luke's. I felt I could never stick it for three years. But I did.'

They had sorted through the old man's clothes. Now they came to a tin box full of papers.

Mary said:

'We must go through these, I suppose.'

They sat down one on each side of the table.

Nurse Hopkins grumbled as she started with a handful.

'Extraordinary what rubbish people keep! Newspaper cuttings! Old letters. All sorts of things!'

Mary said, unfolding a document:

'Here's Dad's and Mum's marriage certificate. At St. Albans, 1919.'

Nurse Hopkins said:

'Marriage lines, that's the old-fashioned term. Lots of the people in this village use that term yet.'

Mary said in a stifled voice:

'But, Nurse——'

'What's the matter?'

Mary Gerrard said in a shaky voice:

'Don't you see? This is 1939. And I'm twenty-one. In 1919 I was a year old. That means—that means—that my father and mother weren't married till—till—*afterwards*.'

Nurse Hopkins frowned. She said robustly:

'Well, after all, what of it? Don't go worrying about that, at *this* time of day!'

'But, Nurse, I can't help it.'

Nurse Hopkins spoke with authority:

'There's many couples that don't go to church till a bit after they should do so. But so long as they do it in the end, what's the odds? That's what I say!'

Mary said in a low voice:

'Is that why—do you think—my father never liked me? Because, perhaps my mother *made* him marry her?'

74

Nurse Hopkins hesitated. She bit her lip, then she said:

'It wasn't quite like that, I imagine.' She paused. 'Oh, well, if you're going to worry about it, you may as well know the truth: You aren't Gerrard's daughter at all.'

Mary said:

'Then *that* was why!'

Nurse Hopkins said: 'Maybe.'

Mary said, a red spot suddenly burning in each cheek:

'I suppose it's wrong of me, but I'm glad! I've always felt uncomfortable because I didn't care for my father, but if he *wasn't* my father, well, that makes it all right! How did you know about it?'

Nurse Hopkins said:

'Gerrard talked about it a good deal before he died. I shut him up pretty sharply, but he didn't care. Naturally, *I* shouldn't have said anything to you about it if this hadn't cropped up.'

Mary said slowly:

'I wonder who my real father was . . .'

Nurse Hopkins hesitated. She opened her mouth, then shut it again. She appeared to be finding it hard to make up her mind on some point.

Then a shadow fell across the room, and the two women looked round to see Elinor Carlisle standing at the window.

Elinor said:

'Good-morning.'

Nurse Hopkins said:

'Good-morning, Miss Carlisle. Lovely day, isn't it?'

Mary said:

'Oh—good-morning, Miss Elinor.'

Elinor said:

'I've been making some sandwiches. Won't you come up and have some? It's just on one o'clock, and it's such a bother to have to go home for lunch. I got enough for three on purpose.'

Nurse Hopkins said in pleased surprise:

'Well, I must say, Miss Carlisle, that's extremely thoughtful of you. It *is* a nuisance to have to break off what you're doing and come all the way back from the village. I hoped we might finish this morning. I went round and saw my cases early. But, there, turning out takes you longer than you think.'

Mary said gratefully:

'Thank you, Miss Elinor, it's very kind of you.'

The three of them walked up the drive to the house. Elinor

had left the front door open. They passed inside into the cool of the hall. Mary shivered a little. Elinor looked at her sharply.

She said:

'What is it?'

Mary said:

'Oh, nothing—just a shiver. It was coming in—out of the sun. . . .'

Elinor said in a low voice:

'That's queer. That's what I felt this morning.'

Nurse Hopkins said in a loud, cheerful voice and with a laugh:

'Come, now, you'll be pretending there are ghosts in the house next. *I* didn't feel anything!'

Elinor smiled. She led the way into the morning-room on the right of the front door. The blinds were up and the windows open. It looked cheerful.

Elinor went across the hall and brought back from the pantry a big plate of sandwiches. She handed it to Mary, saying:

'Have one?'

Mary took one. Elinor stood watching her for a moment as the girl's even white teeth bit into the sandwich.

She held her breath for a minute, then expelled it in a little sigh.

Absent-mindedly she stood for a minute with the plate held to her waist, then at sight of Nurse Hopkins' slightly parted lips and hungry expression she flushed and quickly proffered the plate to the older woman.

Elinor took a sandwich herself. She said apologetically:

'I meant to make some coffee, but I forgot to get any. There's some beer on that table, though, if anyone likes that?'

Nurse Hopkins said sadly:

'If only I'd thought to bring along some tea now.'

Elinor said absently:

'There's a little tea still in the canister in the pantry.'

Nurse Hopkins' face brightened.

'Then I'll just pop out and put the kettle on. No milk, I suppose?'

Elinor said:

'Yes, I brought some.'

'Well, then, that's all right,' said Nurse Hopkins and hurried out.

Elinor and Mary were alone together.

A queer tension crept into the atmosphere. Elinor, with an obvious effort, tried to make conversation. Her lips were dry. She passed her tongue over them. She said, rather stiffly:

'You—like your work in London?'

'Yes, thank you. I—I'm very grateful to you——'

A sudden harsh sound broke from Elinor. A laugh so discordant, so unlike her that Mary stared at her in surprise.

Elinor said:

'You needn't be so grateful!'

Mary, rather embarrassed, said:

'I didn't mean—that is——'

She stopped.

Elinor was staring at her—a glance so searching, so, yes, strange that Mary flinched under it.

She said:

'Is—is anything wrong?'

Elinor got up quickly. She said, turning away:

'What should be wrong?'

Mary murmured:

'You—you looked——'

Elinor said with a little laugh:

'Was I staring? I'm so sorry. I do sometimes—when I'm thinking of something else.'

Nurse Hopkins looked in at the door and remarked brightly, 'I've put the kettle on,' and went out again.

Elinor was taken with a sudden fit of laughter.

'Polly put the kettle on, Polly put the kettle on, Polly put the kettle on—we'll all have tea! Do you remember playing that, Mary, when we were children?'

'Yes, indeed I do.'

Elinor said:

'*When we were children. . . .* It's a pity, Mary, isn't it, that one can never go back? . . .'

Mary said:

'Would you like to go back?'

Elinor said with force:

'Yes . . . *yes.* . . .'

Silence fell between them for a little while.

Then Mary said, her face flushing:

'Miss Elinor, you mustn't think——'

She stopped, warned by the sudden stiffening of Elinor's slender figure, the uplifted line of her chin.

Elinor said in a cold, steel-like voice:

'What mustn't I think?'

Mary murmured:

'I—I've forgotten what I was going to say.'

Elinor's body relaxed—as at a danger past.

Nurse Hopkins came in with a tray. On it was a brown tea-pot, and milk and three cups.

She said, quite unconscious of anti-climax:

'Here's the tea!'

She put the tray in front of Elinor. Elinor shook her head.

'I won't have any.'

She pushed the tray along towards Mary.

Mary poured out two cups.

Nurse Hopkins sighed with satisfaction.

'It's nice and strong.'

Elinor got up and moved over to the window. Nurse Hopkins said persuasively:

'Are you sure you won't have a cup, Miss Carlisle? Do you good.'

Elinor murmured, 'No, thank you.'

Nurse Hopkins drained her cup, replaced it in the saucer and murmured:

'I'll just turn off the kettle. I put it on in case we needed to fill up the pot again.'

She bustled out.

Elinor wheeled round from the window.

She said, and her voice was suddenly charged with a desperate appeal:

'Mary . . .'

Mary Gerrard answered quickly:

'Yes?'

Slowly the light died out of Elinor's face. The lips closed. The desperate pleading faded and left a mere mask—frozen and still.

She said:

'Nothing.'

The silence came down heavily on the room.

Mary thought:

'How queer everything is to-day. As though—as though we were waiting for something.'

Elinor moved at last.

She came from the window and picked up the tea-tray, placing on it the empty sandwich plate.

Mary jumped up.

78

'Oh, Miss Elinor, let me.'

Elinor said sharply:

'No, you stay here. I'll do this.'

She carried the tray out of the room. She looked back, once over her shoulder at Mary Gerrard by the window, young and alive and beautiful. . . .

IV

Nurse Hopkins was in the pantry. She was wiping her face with a handkerchief. She looked up sharply as Elinor entered. She said:

'My word, it's hot in here!'

Elinor answered mechanically:

'Yes, the pantry faces south.'

Nurse Hopkins relieved her of the tray.

'You let me wash up, Miss Carlisle. You're not looking quite the thing.'

Elinor said:

'Oh, I'm all right.'

She picked up a dish-cloth.

'I'll dry.'

Nurse Hopkins slipped off her cuffs. She poured hot water from the kettle into the papier-mâché basin.

Elinor said idly, looking at her wrist:

'You've pricked yourself.'

Nurse Hopkins laughed.

'On the rose trellis at the Lodge—a thorn. I'll get it out presently.'

The rose trellis at the Lodge. . . . Memory poured in waves over Elinor. She and Roddy quarrelling—the Wars of the Roses. She and Roddy quarrelling—and making it up. Lovely, laughing, happy days. A sick wave of revulsion passed over her. What had she come to now? What black abyss of hate— of evil . . . She swayed a little as she stood.

She thought:

'I've been mad—quite mad.'

Nurse Hopkins was staring at her curiously.

'Downright odd, she seemed . . .' so ran Nurse Hopkins' narrative later. 'Talking as if she didn't know what she was saying, and her eyes so bright and queer.'

The cups and saucers rattled in the basin. Elinor picked up

an empty fish-paste pot from the table and put it into the basin. As she did so she said, and marvelled at the steadiness of her voice:

'I've sorted out some clothes upstairs, Aunt Laura's things. I thought, perhaps, Nurse, you could advise me where they would be useful in the village.'

Nurse Hopkins said briskly:

'I will indeed. There's Mrs. Parkinson, and old Nellie, and that poor creature who's not quite all there at Ivy Cottage. Be a godsend to them.'

She and Eliner cleared up the pantry. Then they went upstairs together.

In Mrs. Welman's room clothes were folded in neat bundles: underclothing, dresses, and certain articles of handsome clothing, velvet tea-gowns, a musquash coat. The latter, Elinor explained, she thought of giving to Mrs. Bishop. Nurse Hopkins nodded assent.

She noticed that Mrs. Welman's sables were laid on the chest of drawers.

'Going to have them remodelled for herself,' she thought to herself.

She cast a look at the big tallboy. She wondered if Elinor had found that photograph signed 'Lewis,' and what she had made of it, if so.

'Funny,' she thought to herself, 'the way O'Brien's letter crossed mine. I never dreamt a thing like that could happen. Her hitting on that photo just the day I wrote to her about Mrs. Slattery.'

She helped Elinor sort through the clothing and volunteered to tie it up in separate bundles for the different families and see to their distribution herself.

She said:

'I can be getting on with that while Mary goes down to the Lodge and finishes up there. She's only got a box of papers to go through. Where is the girl, by the way? Did she go down to the Lodge?'

Elinor said:

'I left her in the morning-room . . .'

Nurse Hopkins said:

'She'd not be there all this time.' She glanced at her watch. 'Why, it's nearly an hour we've been up here!'

She bustled down the stairs. Elinor followed her.

They went into the morning-room.

Nurse Hopkins exclaimed:

'Well, I never, she's fallen asleep.'

Mary Gerrard was sitting in a big arm-chair by the window. She had dropped down a little in it. There was a queer sound in the room: stertorous, laboured breathing.

Nurse Hopkins went across and shook the girl.

'Wake up, my dear——'

She broke off. She bent lower, pulled down an eyelid. Then she started shaking the girl in grim earnest.

She turned on Elinor. There was something menacing in her voice as she said:

'What's all this?'

Elinor said:

'I don't know what you mean. Is she ill?'

Nurse Hopkins said:

'Where's the phone? Get hold of Dr. Lord as soon as you can.'

Elinor said:

'What's the matter?'

'The matter? The girl's ill. She's dying.'

Elinor recoiled a step.

She said:

'*Dying?*'

Nurse Hopkins said:

'She's been poisoned. . . .'

Her eyes, hard with suspicion, glared at Elinor.

PART TWO

CHAPTER ONE

Hercule Poirot, his egg-shaped head gently tilted to one side, his eyebrows raised inquiringly, his fingertips joined together, watched the young man who was striding so savagely up and down the room, his pleasant freckled face puckered and drawn.

Hercule Poirot said:

'*Eh bien*, my friend, what *is* all this?'

Peter Lord stopped dead in his pacing.

He said:

'M. Poirot. You're the only man in the world who can help me. I've heard Stillingfleet talk about you; he's told me what you did in that Benedict Farley case. How every mortal soul thought it was suicide and you showed that it was murder.'

Hercule Poirot said:

'Have you, then, a case of suicide among your patients about which you are not satisfied?'

Peter Lord shook his head.

He sat down opposite Poirot.

He said:

'There's a young woman. She's been arrested and she's going to be tried for murder! I want you to find evidence that will prove that she didn't do it!'

Poirot's eyebrows rose a little higher. Then he assumed a discreet and confidential manner.

He said:

'You and this young lady—you are affianced—yes? You are in love with each other?'

Peter Lord laughed—a sharp, bitter laugh.

He said:

'No, it's not like that! She has the bad taste to prefer a long-nosed supercilious ass with a face like a melancholy horse! Stupid of her, but there it is!'

Poirot said:

'I see.'

Lord said bitterly:

'Oh, yes, you see all right! No need to be so tactful about it. I fell for her straightaway. And because of that I don't want her hanged. See?'

Poirot said:

'What is the charge against her?'

'She's accused of murdering a girl called Mary Gerrard, by poisoning her with morphine hydrochloride. You've probably read the account of the inquest in the papers.'

Poirot said:

'And the motive?'

'Jealousy!'

'And in your opinion she didn't do it?'

'No, of course not.'

Hercule Poirot looked at him thoughtfully for a moment or two, then he said:

'What is it exactly that you want me to do? To investigate this matter?'

'I want you to get her off.'

'I am not a defending counsel, *mon cher*.'

'I'll put it more clearly: *I want you to find evidence that will enable her counsel to get her off.*'

Hercule Poirot said:

'You put this a little curiously.'

Peter Lord said:

'Because I don't wrap it up, you mean? It seems simple enough to me. *I want this girl acquitted.* I think *you* are the only man who can do it!'

'You wish me to look into the facts? To find out the truth? To discover what really happened?'

'I want you to find any facts that will tell in her favour.'

Hercule Poirot, with care and precision, lighted a very tiny cigarette. He said:

'But is it not a little unethical what you say there? To arrive at the truth, yes, that always interests me. But the truth is a two-edged weapon. Supposing that I find facts *against* the lady? Do you demand that I suppress them?'

Peter Lord stood up. He was very white. He said:

'That's impossible! Nothing that you could find could be more against her than the facts are already! They're utterly and completely damning! There's any amount of evidence against her black and plain for all the world to see! You couldn't find anything that would damn her more completely than she is already! I'm asking you to use all your ingenuity

—Stillfleet says you're damned ingenious—to ferret out a loophole, a possible alternative.'

Hercule Poirot said:

'Surely her lawyers will do that?'

'Will they?' the young man laughed scornfully. 'They're licked before they start! Think it's hopeless! They've briefed Bulmer, K.C.—the forlorn hope man; that's a give-away in itself! Big orator—sob stuff—stressing the prisoner's youth— all that! But the judge won't let him get away with it. Not a hope!'

Hercule Poirot said:

'Supposing she *is* guilty—do you still want to get her acquitted?'

Peter Lord said quietly:

'Yes.'

Hercule Poirot moved in his chair. He said:

'You interest me. . . .'

After a minute or two he said:

'You had better, I think, tell me the exact facts of the case.'

'Haven't you read anything about it in the papers?'

Hercule Poirot waved a hand.

'A mention of it—yes. But the newspapers, they are so inaccurate. I never go by what they say.'

Peter Lord said:

'It's quite simple. Horribly simple. This girl, Elinor Carlisle, had just come into a place near here—Hunterbury Hall—and a fortune from her aunt, who died intestate. Aunt's name was Welman. Aunt had a nephew by marriage Roderick Welman. He was engaged to Elinor Carlisle—long-standing business, known each other since children. There was a girl down at Hunterbury: Mary Gerrard, daughter of the lodge-keeper. Old Mrs. Welman had made a lot of fuss about her, paid for her education, etc. Consequence is, girl was to outward seeming a lady. Roderick Welman, it seems, fell for her. In consequence, engagement was broken off.

'Now we come to the doings. Elinor Carlisle put up the place for sale and a man called Somervell bought it. Elinor came down to clear out her aunt's personal possessions and so on. Mary Gerrard, whose father had just died, was clearing out the Lodge. That brings us to the morning of July 27th.

'Elinor Carlisle was staying at the local pub. In the street she met the former housekeeper, Mrs. Bishop. Mrs. Bishop suggested coming up to the house to help her. Elinor refused—

rather over-vehemently. Then she went into the grocer's shop and bought some fish paste, and there she made a remark about food-poisoning. You see? Perfectly innocent thing to do; but, of course, it tells against her! She went up to the house, and about one o'clock she went down to the Lodge, where Mary Gerrard was busy with the District Nurse, a Nosey Parker of a woman called Hopkins, helping her, and told them that she had some sandwiches ready up at the house. They came up to the house with her, ate sandwiches, and about an hour or so later I was sent for and found Mary Gerrard unconscious. Did all I could, but it was no good. Autopsy revealed large dose of morphine had been taken a short time previously. And the police found a scrap of a label with morphia hydrochlor on it just where Elinor Carlisle had been spreading the sandwiches.'

'What else did Mary Gerrard eat or drink?'

'She and the District Nurse drank tea with the sandwiches. Nurse made it and Mary poured it out. Couldn't have been anything there. Of course, I understand Counsel will make a song and dance about sandwiches, too, saying all three ate them, therefore *impossible* to ensure that only one person should be poisoned. They said that in the Hearne case, you remember.'

Poirot nodded. He said:

'But actually it is very simple. You make your pile of sandwiches. *In one of them is the poison.* You hand the plate. In our state of civilisation it is a foregone conclusion that the person to whom the plate is offered will take *the sandwich that is nearest to them.* I presume that Elinor Carlisle handed the plate to Mary Gerrard first?'

'Exactly.'

'Although the nurse, who was an older woman, was in the room?'

'Yes.'

'That does not look very good.'

'It doesn't mean a thing, really. You don't stand on ceremony at a picnic lunch.'

'Who cut the sandwiches?'

'Elinor Carlisle.'

'Was there anyone else in the house?'

'No one.'

Poirot shook his head.

'It is bad, that. And the girl had *nothing* but the tea and the sandwiches?'

'Nothing. Stomach contents tell us that.'

Poirot said:

'It is suggested that Elinor Carlisle hoped the girl's death would be taken for food poisoning? How did she propose to explain the fact that only *one* member of the party was affected?'

Peter Lord said:

'It does happen that way sometimes. Also, there were two pots of paste—both much alike in appearance. The idea would be that one pot was all right and that by a coincidence all the bad paste was eaten by Mary.'

'An interesting study in the laws of probability,' said Poirot. 'The mathematical chances against that happening would be high, I fancy. But another point, if food poisoning was to be suggested: *Why not choose a different poison?* The symptoms of morphine are not in the least like those of food poisoning. Atropine, surely, would have been a better choice!'

Peter Lord said slowly:

'Yes, that's true. But there's something more. That damned District Nurse swears she lost a tube of morphine!'

'When?'

'Oh, weeks earlier, the night old Mrs. Welman died. The nurse says she left her case in the hall and found a tube of morphine missing in the morning. All bunkum, I believe. Probably smashed it at home some time before and forgot about it.'

'She has only remembered it *since* the death of Mary Gerrard?'

Peter Lord said reluctantly:

'As a matter of fact, she *did* mention it at the time—to the nurse on duty.'

Hercule Poirot was looking at Peter Lord with some interest.

He said gently:

'I think, *mon cher*, there is something else—something that you have not yet told me.'

Peter Lord said:

'Oh, well, I suppose you'd better have it all. They're applying for an exhumation order and going to dig up old Mrs. Welman.'

Poirot said:

'*Eh bien?*'

Peter Lord said:

'When they do, *they'll probably find what they're looking for—morphine!*'

'You knew that?'

Peter Lord, his face white under the freckles, muttered:

'I suspected it.'

Hercule Poirot beat with his hand on the arm of his chair. He cried out:

'*Mon Dieu*, I do not understand you! You *knew* when she died that she had been murdered?'

Peter Lord shouted:

'Good lord, no! I never dreamt of such a thing! I thought she'd taken it herself.'

Poirot sank back in his chair.

'Ah! You thought *that*. . . .'

'Of course I did! She'd talked to me about it. Asked me more than once if I couldn't "finish her off." She hated illness, the helplessness of it—the—what she called the *indignity* of lying there tended like a baby. And she was a very determined woman.'

He was silent a moment, then he went on:

'I was surprised at her death. I hadn't expected it. I sent the nurse out of the room and made as thorough an investigation as I could. Of course, it was impossible to be sure without an autopsy. Well, what was the good of that? *If* she'd taken a short-cut, why make a song and dance about it and create a scandal? Better sign the certificate and let her be buried in peace. After all, I couldn't be sure. I decided wrong, I suppose. But I never dreamed for one moment of foul play. I was quite sure she'd done it herself.'

Poirot asked:

'How do you think she had got hold of the morphine?'

'I hadn't the least idea. But, as I tell you, she was a clever, resourceful woman, with plenty of ingenuity and remarkable determination.'

'Would she have got it from the nurses?'

Peter Lord shook his head.

'Never on your life! You don't know nurses!'

'From her family?'

'Possibly. Might have worked on their feelings.'

Hercule Poirot said:

'You have told me that Mrs. Welman died intestate. If she had lived, would she have made a will?'

Peter Lord grinned suddenly.

'Putting your finger with fiendish accuracy on all the vital spots, aren't you? Yes, she was going to make a will; very agitated about it. Couldn't speak intelligently, but made her wishes clear. Elinor Carlisle was to have telephoned the lawyer first thing in the morning.'

'So Elinor Carlisle knew that her aunt wanted to make a will? And if her aunt died without making one, Elinor Carlisle inherited everything?'

Peter Lord said quickly:

'She didn't know that. She'd no idea her aunt had never made a will.'

'That, my friend, is what she *says*. She *may* have known.'

'Look here, Poirot, are you the Prosecuting Counsel?'

'At the moment, yes. I must know the full strength of the case against her. Could Elinor Carlisle have taken the morphine from the attaché-case?'

'Yes. So could anyone else. Roderick Welman. Nurse O'Brien. Any of the servants.'

'Or Dr. Lord?'

Peter Lord's eyes opened wide. He said:

'Certainly. . . . But what would be the idea?'

'Mercy, perhaps.'

Peter Lord shook his head.

'Nothing doing there! You'll have to believe me!'

Hercule Poirot leaned back in his chair. He said:

'Let us entertain a supposition. Let us say that Elinor Carlisle did take that morphine from the attaché-case and did administer it to her aunt. Was anything said about the loss of the morphine?'

'Not to the household. The two nurses kept it to themselves.'

Poirot said:

'What, in your opinion, will be the action of the Crown?'

'You mean if they find morphine in Mrs. Welman's body?'

'Yes.'

Peter Lord said grimly:

'It's possible that if Elinor is acquitted of the present charge she will be rearrested and charged with the murder of her aunt.'

Poirot said thoughtfully:

'The motives are different; that is to say, in the case of Mrs. Welman the motive would have been *gain*, whereas in the case of Mary Gerrard the motive is supposed to be *jealousy*.'

'That's right.'

Poirot said:

'What line does the defence propose to take?'

Peter Lord said:

'Bulmer proposes to take the line that there was no motive. He'll put forward the theory that the engagement between Elinor and Roderick was a family business, entered into for family reasons, to please Mrs. Welman, and that the moment the old lady was dead Elinor broke it off of her own accord. Roderick Welman will give evidence to that effect. I think he almost believes it!'

'Believes that Elinor did not care for him to any great extent?'

'Yes.'

'In which case,' said Poirot, 'she would have no reason for murdering Mary Gerrard.'

'Exactly.'

'But in that case, who *did* murder Mary Gerrard?'

'As you say.'

Poirot shook his head.

'*C'est difficile.*'

Peter Lord said vehemently:

'That's just it! If *she* didn't, *who did*? There's the tea; but both Nurse Hopkins and Mary drank that. The defence will try and suggest that Mary Gerrard took the morphine herself after the other two had left the room—that she committed suicide, in fact.'

'Had she any reason for committing suicide?'

'None whatever.'

'Was she of a suicidal type?'

'No.'

Poirot said:

'What was she like, this Mary Gerrard?'

Peter Lord considered:

'She was—well, she was a nice kid. Yes, definitely a nice kid.'

Poirot sighed. He murmured:

'This Roderick Welman, did he fall in love with her because she was a nice kid?'

Peter Lord smiled.

'Oh, I get what you mean. She was beautiful, all right.'

'And you yourself? You had no feeling for her?'

Peter Lord stared.

'Good lord, no.'

Hercule Poirot reflected for a moment or two, then he said:

'Roderick Welman says that there was affection between him and Elinor Carlisle, but nothing stronger. Do you agree to that?'

'How the hell should I know?'

Poirot shook his head.

'You told me when you came into this room that Elinor Carlisle had the bad taste to be in love with a long-nosed, supercilious ass. That, I presume, is a description of Roderick Welman. So, according to you, she *does* care for him.'

Peter Lord said in a low, exasperated voice:

'She cares for him all right! Cares like hell!'

Poirot said:

'Then there *was* a motive. . . .'

Peter Lord swerved round on him, his face alight with anger.

'Does it matter? She might have done it, yes! *I don't care if she did.*'

Poirot said:

'Aha!'

'But I don't want her hanged, I tell you! Supposing she *was* driven desperate? Love's a desperate and twisting business. It can turn a worm into a fine fellow—and it can bring a decent, straight man down to the dregs! Suppose she *did* do it. Haven't you got any pity?'

Hercule Poirot said:

'I do not approve of murder.'

Peter Lord stared at him, looked away, stared again and finally burst out laughing.

'Of all the things to say—so prim and smug, too! Who's asking you to approve? I'm not asking you to tell lies! Truth's truth, isn't it? If you find something that tells in an accused person's favour, you wouldn't be inclined to suppress it because she's guilty, would you?'

'Certainly not.'

'Then why the hell can't you do what I ask you?'

Hercule Poirot said:

'My friend, I am perfectly prepared to do so. . . .'

CHAPTER TWO

Peter Lord stared at him, took out a handkerchief, wiped his face and threw himself down in a chair.

'Whoof!' he said. 'You got me all worked up! I didn't see in the least what you were getting at!'

Poirot said:

'I was examining the case against Elinor Carlisle. Now I know it. Morphine was administered to Mary Gerrard; and, as far as I can see, it *must* have been given in the sandwiches. Nobody touched those sandwiches *except Elinor Carlisle*. Elinor Carlisle had a *motive* for killing Mary Gerrard, and she is, in your opinion, *capable* of killing Mary Gerrard, and in all probability she *did* kill Mary Gerrard. I see no reason for believing otherwise.

'That, *mon ami*, is one side of the question. Now we will proceed to stage two. We will dismiss all those considerations from our mind and we will approach the matter from the opposite angle: *If Elinor Carlisle did not kill Mary Gerrard, who did?* Or did Mary Gerrard commit suicide?'

Peter Lord sat up. A frown creased his forehead. He said:

'You weren't quite accurate just now.'

'I? *Not accurate?*'

Poirot sounded affronted.

Peter Lord pursued relentlessly:

'No. You said nobody but Elinor Carlisle touched those sandwiches. You don't know that.'

'There was no one else in the house.'

'*As far as we know.* But you are excluding a short period of time. *There was a time during which Elinor Carlisle left the house to go down to the Lodge.* During that period of time the sandwiches were on a plate in the pantry, and somebody *could* have tampered with them.'

Poirot drew a deep breath.

He said:

'You are right, my friend. I admit it. There *was* a time during which somebody could have had access to the plate of sandwiches. We must try to form some idea *who that some-*

body could be; that is to say, *what kind of person. . . .*'

He paused.

'Let us consider this Mary Gerrard. *Someone*, not Elinor Carlisle, desires her death. *Why?* Did anyone stand to gain by her death? Had she money to leave?'

Peter Lord shook his head.

'Not now. In another month she would have had two thousand pounds. Elinor Carlisle was making that sum over to her because she believed her aunt would have wished it. But the old lady's estate isn't wound up yet.'

Poirot said:

'Then we can wash out the money angle. Mary Gerrard was beautiful, you say. With that there are always complications. She had admirers?'

'Probably. I don't know much about it.'

'Who would know?'

Peter Lord grinned.

'I'd better put you on to Nurse Hopkins. She's the town crier. She knows everything that goes on in Maidensford.'

'I was going to ask you to give me your impressions of the two nurses.'

'Well, O'Brien's Irish, good nurse, competent, a bit silly, could be spiteful, a bit of a liar—the imaginative kind that's not so much deceitful, but just has to make a good story out of everything.'

Poirot nodded.

'Hopkins is a sensible, shrewd, middle-aged woman, quite kindly and competent, but a sight too much interested in other people's business!'

'If there had been trouble over some young man in the village, would Nurse Hopkins know about it?'

'You bet!'

He added slowly:

'All the same, I don't believe there can be anything very obvious in that line. Mary hadn't been home long. She'd been away in Germany for two years.'

'She was twenty-one?'

'Yes.'

'There may be some German complication.'

Peter Lord's face brightened.

He said eagerly:

'You mean that some German fellow may have had it in for her? He may have followed her over here, waited his time,

93

and finally achieved his object?'

'It sounds a little melodramatic,' said Hercule Poirot doubtfully.

'But it's *possible*?'

'Not very probable, though.'

Peter Lord said:

'I don't agree. Someone *might* get all het up about the girl, and see red when she turned him down. He may have fancied she treated him badly. It's an idea.'

'It is an idea, yes,' said Hercule Poirot, but his tone was not encouraging.

Peter Lord said pleadingly:

'Go on, M. Poirot.'

'You want me, I see, to be the conjurer. To take out of the empty hat rabbit after rabbit.'

'You can put it that way if you like.'

'There *is* another possibility,' said Hercule Poirot.

'Go on.'

'*Someone* abstracted a tube of morphine from Nurse Hopkins' case that evening in June. *Suppose Mary Gerrard saw the person who did it?*'

'She would have said so.'

'No, no, *mon cher*. Be reasonable. If Elinor Carlisle, or Roderick Welman, or Nurse O'Brien, or even any of the servants, were to open that case and abstract a little glass tube, what would anyone think? Simply that the person in question had been sent by the nurse to fetch something from it. The matter would pass straight out of Mary Gerrard's mind again, but it is possible that, later, she *might* recollect the fact and might mention it casually to the person in question—oh, without the least suspicion in the world. But to the person guilty of the murder of Mrs. Welman, imagine the effect of that remark! Mary had seen: Mary must be silenced at all costs! I can assure you, my friend, that anyone who has once committed a murder finds it only too easy to commit another!'

Peter Lord said with a frown:

'I've believed all along that Mrs. Welman took the stuff herself. . . .'

'But she was paralysed—helpless—she had just had a second stroke.'

'Oh, I know. My idea was that, having got hold of morphine somehow or other, she kept it by her in a receptacle close at hand.'

'But in that case she must have got hold of the morphine *before* her second attack and the nurse missed it afterwards.'

'Hopkins may only have missed the morphine that morning. It might have been *taken* a couple of days before, and she hadn't noticed it.'

'How would the old lady have got hold of it?'

'I don't know. Bribed a servant, perhaps. If so, that servant's never going to tell.'

'You don't think either of the nurses were bribable?'

Lord shook his head.

'Not on your life! To begin with, they're both very strict about their professional ethics—and in addition they'd be scared to death to do such a thing. They'd know the danger to themselves.'

Poirot said:

'That is so.'

He added thoughtfully:

'It looks, does it not, as though we return to our muttons? Who is the most likely person to have taken that morphine tube? *Elinor Carlisle.* We may say that she wished to make sure of inheriting a large fortune. We may be more generous and say that she was actuated by pity, that she took the morphine and administered it in compliance with her aunt's often-repeated request; but *she* took it—*and Mary Gerrard saw her do it.* And so we are back at the sandwiches and the empty house, and we have Elinor Carlisle once more—but this time with a different motive: to save her neck.'

Peter Lord cried out:

'That's fantastic. I tell you, she isn't that kind of person! Money doesn't really mean anything to her—or to Roderick Welman, either, I'm bound to admit. I've heard them both say as much!'

'You have? That is very interesting. That is the kind of statement I always look upon with a good deal of suspicion myself.'

Peter Lord said:

'Damn you, Poirot, must you always twist everything round so that it comes back to that girl?'

'It is not I that twist things round: they come round of themselves. It is like the pointer at the fair. It swings round, and when it comes to rest it points always at the same name—*Elinor Carlisle.*'

Peter Lord said:

'No!'

Hercule Poirot shook his head sadly.

Then he said:

'Has she relations, this Elinor Carlisle? Sisters, cousins? A father or mother?'

'No. She's an orphan—alone in the world . . .'

'How pathetic it sounds! Bulmer, I am sure, will make great play with that! Who, then, inherits her money if she dies?'

'I don't know. I haven't thought.'

Poirot said reprovingly:

'One should always think of these things. Has she made a will, for instance?'

Peter Lord flushed. He said uncertainly:

'I—I don't know.'

Hercule Poirot looked at the ceiling and joined his finger-tips.

He remarked:

'It would be well, you know, to tell me.'

'Tell you what?'

'Exactly what is in your mind—no matter how damaging it may happen to be to Elinor Carlisle.'

'How do you know——?'

'Yes, yes, I know. There is *something*—some incident in your mind! It will be as well to tell me, otherwise I shall imagine it is something worse than it is!'

'It's nothing, really——'

'We will agree it is nothing. But let me hear what it is.'

Slowly, unwillingly, Peter Lord allowed the story to be dragged from him—that scene of Elinor leaning in at the window of Nurse Hopkins' cottage, and of her laughter.

Poirot said thoughtfully:

'She said that, did she, "*So you're making your will, Mary? That's funny—that's very funny.*" And it was very clear to you what was in her mind. . . . She had been thinking, perhaps, *that Mary Gerrard was not going to live long. . . .*'

Peter Lord said:

'I only imagined that. I don't know.'

Poirot said:

'No, you did not only imagine it . . .'

CHAPTER THREE

Hercule Poirot sat in Nurse Hopkins' cottage.

Dr. Lord had brought him there, had introduced him and had then, at a glance from Poirot, left him to a tête-à-tête.

Having, to begin with, eyed his foreign appearance somewhat askance, Nurse Hopkins was now thawing rapidly.

She said with a faintly gloomy relish:

'Yes, it's a terrible thing. One of the most terrible things I've ever known. Mary was one of the most beautiful girls you've ever seen. Might have gone on the films any time! And a nice steady girl, too, and not stuck-up, as she might have been with all the notice taken of her.'

Poirot, inserting a question adroitly, said:

'You mean the notice taken of her by Mrs. Welman?'

'That's what I mean. The old lady had taken a tremendous fancy to her—really, a tremendous fancy.'

Hercule Poirot murmured:

'Surprising, perhaps?'

'That depends. It might be quite natural, really. I mean . . .' Nurse Hopkins bit her lip and looked confused. 'What I mean is, Mary had a very pretty way with her: nice soft voice and pleasant manners. And it's my opinion it does an elderly person good to have a young face about.'

Hercule Poirot said:

'Miss Carlisle came down occasionally, I suppose, to see her aunt?'

Nurse Hopkins said sharply:

'Miss Carlisle came down when it suited her.'

Poirot murmured:

'You do not like Miss Carlisle.'

Nurse Hopkins cried out:

'I should hope not, indeed! A poisoner! A cold-blooded poisoner!'

'Ah,' said Hercule Poirot, 'I see you have made up your mind.'

Nurse Hopkins said suspiciously:

'What do you mean? Made up my mind?'

'You are quite sure that it was she who administered morphine to Mary Gerrard?'

'Who else could have done it, I should like to know? You're not suggesting that *I* did?'

'Not for a moment. But her guilt has not yet been proved, remember.'

Nurse Hopkins said with calm assurance:

'She did it all right. Apart from anything else, you could see it in her face. Queer she was, all the time. And taking me away upstairs and keeping me there—delaying as long as possible. And then when I turned on her, after finding Mary like that, it was there in her face as plain as anything. She knew I knew!'

Hercule Poirot said thoughtfully:

'It is certainly difficult to see who else could have done it. Unless of course, she did it herself.'

'What do you mean, *did it herself*? Do you mean that Mary committed suicide? I never heard such nonsense!'

Hercule Poirot said:

'One can never tell. The heart of a young girl, it is very sensitive, very tender.' He paused. 'It would have been possible, I suppose? She could have slipped something into her tea without your noticing her?'

'Slipped it into her cup, you mean?'

'Yes. You weren't watching her all the time.'

'I wasn't watching her—no. Yes, I suppose she *could* have done that. . . . But it's all nonsense! What would she want to do a thing like that for?'

Hercule Poirot shook his head with a resumption of his former manner.

'A young girl's heart . . . as I say, so sensitive. An unhappy love-affair, perhaps——'

Nurse Hopkins gave a snort.

'Girls don't kill themselves for love-affairs—not unless they're in the family way—and Mary wasn't *that*, let me tell you!' She glared at him belligerently.

'And she was not in love?'

'Not she. Quite fancy free. Keen on her job and enjoying her life.'

'But she must have had admirers, since she was such an attractive girl.'

Nurse Hopkins said:

'She wasn't one of these girls who are all S.A. and IT. She

98

was a quiet girl!'

'But there were young men, no doubt, in the village who admired her.'

'There was Ted Bigland, of course,' said Nurse Hopkins.

Poirot extracted various details as to Ted Bigland.

'Very gone on Mary, he was,' said Nurse Hopkins. 'But, as I told her, she was a cut above him.'

Poirot said:

'He must have been angry when she would not have anything to do with him?'

'He was sore about it, yes,' admitted Nurse Hopkins. 'Blamed *me* for it, too.'

'He thought it was your fault?'

'That's what he said. I'd a perfect right to advise the girl. After all, I know something of the world. I didn't want the girl to throw herself away.'

Poirot said gently:

'What made you take so much interest in the girl?'

'Well, I don't know . . .' Nurse Hopkins hesitated. She looked shy and a little ashamed of herself. 'There was something—well—romantic about Mary.'

Poirot murmured:

'About *her*, perhaps, but not about her circumstances. She was the lodge-keeper's daughter, wasn't she?'

Nurse Hopkins said:

'Yes—yes, of course. At least——'

She hesitated, looked at Poirot, who was gazing at her in the most sympathetic manner.

'As a matter of fact,' said Nurse Hopkins, in a burst of confidence, 'she wasn't old Gerrard's daughter at all. He told me so. Her father was a gentleman.'

Poirot murmured:

'I see . . . And her mother?'

Nurse Hopkins hesitated, bit her lip, and then went on:

'Her mother had been lady's maid to old Mrs. Welman. She married Gerrard after Mary was born.'

'As you say, quite a romance—a mystery romance.'

Nurse Hopkins' face lit up.

'Wasn't it? One can't help taking an interest in people when one knows something that nobody else does about them. Just by chance I happened to find out a good deal. As a matter of fact, it was Nurse O'Brien who set me on the track; but that's another story. But, as you say, it's interesting knowing past history. There's many a tragedy that goes unguessed at. It's a sad world.'

Poirot sighed and shook his head.

Nurse Hopkins said with sudden alarm:

'But I oughtn't to have gone talking like this. I wouldn't have a word of this get out for anything! After all, it's nothing to do with the case. As far as the world is concerned, Mary was Gerrard's daughter, and there mustn't be a hint of anything else. Damaging her in the eyes of the world after she's dead! He married her mother, and that's enough.'

Poirot murmured:

'But you know, perhaps, who her real father was?'

Nurse Hopkins said reluctantly:

'Well, perhaps I do; but, then again, perhaps I don't. That is, I don't *know* anything. I could make a guess. Old sins have long shadows, as they say! But I'm not one to talk, and I shan't say another word.'

Poirot tactfully retired from the fray and attacked another subject.

'There is something else—a delicate matter. But I am sure I can rely on your discretion.'

Nurse Hopkins bridled. A broad smile appeared on her homely face.

Poirot continued:

'I speak of Mr. Roderick Welman. He was, so I hear, attracted by Mary Gerrard.'

Nurse Hopkins said:

'Bowled over by her!'

'Although at the time he was engaged to Miss Carlisle?'

'If you ask me,' said Nurse Hopkins, 'he was never really sweet on Miss Carlisle. Not what I'd call *sweet* on her.'

Poirot asked, using an old-fashioned term:

'Did Mary Gerrard—er—encourage his advances?'

Nurse Hopkins said sharply:

'She behaved very well. Nobody could say she led him on!'

Poirot said:

'Was she in love with him?'

Nurse Hopkins said sharply:

'No, she wasn't.'

'But she liked him?'

'Oh, yes, she *liked* him well enough.'

'And I suppose, in time, something might have come of it?'

Nurse Hopkins admitted that,

100

'That may be. But Mary wouldn't have done anything in a hurry. She told him down here he had no business to speak like that to her when he was engaged to Miss Elinor. And when he came to see her in London she said the same.'

Poirot asked with an air of engaging candour:

'What do you think yourself of Mr. Roderick Welman?'

Nurse Hopkins said:

'He's a nice enough young fellow. Nervy, though. Looks as though he might be dyspeptic later on. Those nervy ones often are.'

'Was he very fond of his aunt?'

'I believe so.'

'Did he sit with her much when she was so ill?'

'You mean when she had that second stroke? The night before she died when they came down? I don't believe he even went into her room!'

'Really.'

Nurse Hopkins said quickly:

'She didn't ask for him. And, of course, we'd no idea the end was so near. There are a lot of men like that, you know: fight shy of a sick-room. They can't help it. And it's not heartlessness. They just don't want to be upset in their feelings.'

Poirot nodded comprehendingly.

He said:

'Are you *sure* Mr. Welman did not go into his aunt's room before she died?'

'Well not while *I* was on duty! Nurse O'Brien relieved me at 3 a.m., and she may have fetched him before the end; but, it so, she didn't mention it to me.'

Poirot suggested:

'He may have gone into her room when you were absent?'

Nurse Hopkins snapped:

'I don't leave my patients unattended, Mr. Poirot.'

'A thousand apologies. I did not mean that. I thought perhaps you might have had to boil water, or to run downstairs for some necessary stimulant.'

Mollified, Nurse Hopkins said:

'I did go down to change the bottles and get them refilled. I knew there'd be a kettle on the boil down in the kitchen.'

'You were away long?'

'Five minutes, perhaps.'

'Ah, yes, then Mr. Welman *may* have just looked in on her then?'

'He must have been very quick about it if he did.'

Poirot sighed. He said:

'As you say, men fight shy of illness. It is the women who are the ministering angels. What should we do without them? Especially women of your profession—a truly noble calling.'

Nurse Hopkins, slightly red in the face, said:

'It's very kind of you to say that. I've never thought of it that way myself. Too much hard work in nursing to think about the noble side of it.'

Poirot said:

'And there is nothing else you can tell me about Mary Gerrard?'

There was an appreciable pause before Nurse Hopkins answered:

'I don't know of anything.'

'Are you quite sure?'

Nurse Hopkins said rather incoherently:

'You don't understand. I was *fond* of Mary.'

'And there is nothing more you can tell me?'

'No, there is not! And that's flat.'

CHAPTER FOUR

In the awesome majesty of Mrs. Bishop's black-clad presence Hercule Poirot sat humbly insignificant.

The thawing of Mrs. Bishop was no easy matter. For Mrs. Bishop, a lady of Conservative habits and views, strongly disapproved of foreigners. And a foreigner most indubitably Hercule Poirot was. Her responses were frosty and she eyed him with disfavour and suspicion.

Dr. Lord's introduction of him had done little to soften the situation.

'I am sure,' said Mrs. Bishop when Dr. Lord had gone, 'Dr. Lord is a very clever doctor and means well. Dr. Ransome, his predecessor, had been here *many* years!'

Dr. Ransome, that is to say, could be trusted to behave in a manner suitable to the county. Dr. Lord, a mere irresponsible youngster, an upstart who had taken Dr. Ransome's place, had only one recommendation: 'cleverness' in his profession.

Cleverness, the whole demeanour of Mrs. Bishop seemed to say, is not enough!

Hercule Poirot was persuasive. He was adroit. But charm he never so wisely, Mrs. Bishop remained aloof and implacable.

The death of Mrs. Welman had been very sad. She had been much respected in the neighbourhood. The arrest of Miss Carlisle was 'Disgraceful!' and believed to be the result of 'these new-fangled police methods.' The views of Mrs. Bishop upon the death of Mary Gerrard were vague in the extreme. 'I couldn't say, I'm sure,' being the most she could be brought to say.

Hercule Poirot played his last card. He recounted with naïve pride a recent visit of his to Sandringham. He spoke with admiration of the graciousness and delightful simplicity and kindness of Royalty.

Mrs. Bishop, who followed daily in the court circular the exact movements of Royalty, was overborne. After all, if They had sent for Mr. Poirot ... Well, naturally, that made All the Difference. Foreigner or no foreigner, who was she, Emma Bishop, to hold back where Royalty had led the way?

Presently she and M. Poirot were engaged in pleasant conversation on a really interesting theme—no less than the selection of a suitable future husband for Princess Elizabeth.

Having finally exhausted all possible candidates as Not Good Enough, the talk reverted to less exalted circles.

Poirot observed sententiously:

'Marriage, alas, is fraught with dangers and pitfalls!'

Mrs. Bishop said:

'Yes, indeed—with this nasty divorce,' rather as though she were speaking of a contagious disease such as chickenpox.

'I expect,' said Poirot, 'that Mrs. Welman, before her death, must have been anxious to see her niece suitably settled in life?'

Mrs. Bishop bowed her head.

'Yes, indeed. The engagement between Miss Elinor and Mr. Roderick was a great relief to her. It was a thing she had always hoped for.'

Poirot ventured:

'The engagement was perhaps entered into partly from a wish to please her?'

'Oh, no, I wouldn't say *that*, Mr. Poirot. Miss Elinor has always been devoted to Mr. Roddy—always was, as a tiny tot—quite beautiful to see. Miss Elinor has a very loyal and devoted nature!'

Poirot murmured:

'And he?'

Mrs. Bishop said austerely:

'Mr. Roderick was devoted to Miss Elinor.'

Poirot said:

'Yet the engagement, I think, was broken off?'

The colour rose in Mrs. Bishop's face. She said:

'Owing, Mr. Poirot, to the machinations of a snake in the grass.'

Poirot said, appearing suitably impressed:

'Indeed?'

Mrs. Bishop, her face becoming redder still, explained:

'In this country, Mr. Poirot, there is a certain Decency to be observed when mentioning the Dead. But that young woman, Mr. Poirot, was Underhand in her Dealings.'

Poirot looked at her thoughtfully for a moment.

Then he said with an apparent lack of guile:

'You surprise me. I had been given the impression that she was a very simple and unassuming girl.'

Mrs. Bishop's chin trembled a little.

'She was Artful, Mr. Poirot. People were Taken In by her. That Nurse Hopkins, for instance! Yes, and my poor dear mistress, too!'

Poirot shook his head sympathetically and made a clacking noise with his tongue.

'Yes, indeed,' said Mrs. Bishop, stimulated by these encouraging noises. 'She was failing, poor dear, and that young woman Wormed her way into her Confidence. *She* knew which side of her bread was buttered. Always hovering about, reading to her, bringing her little nosegays of flowers. It was Mary this and Mary that and "Where's Mary?" all the time! The money she spent on the girl, too! Expensive schools and finishing places abroad—and the girl nothing but old Gerrard's daughter! *He* didn't like it, I can tell you! Used to complain of her Fine Lady ways. Above Herself, that's what *She* was.'

This time Poirot shook his head and said commiseratingly:

'Dear, dear.'

'And then Making Up to Mr. Roddy the way she did! He

104

was too simple to see through Her. And Miss Elinor, a nice-minded young lady as she is, of course she wouldn't realise what was Going On. But Men, they are all alike: easily caught by flattery and a pretty face!'

Poirot sighed.

'She had, I suppose, admirers of her own class?' he asked.

'Of course she had. There was Rufus Bigland's son Ted—as nice a boy as you could find. But oh, no, my fine lady was too good for *him*! I'd no patience with such airs and graces!'

Poirot said:

'Was he not angry about her treatment of him?'

'Yes, indeed. He accused her of carrying on with Mr. Roddy. I know *that* for a *fact*. I don't blame the boy for feeling sore!'

'Nor I,' said Poirot. 'You interest me extremely, Mrs. Bishop. Some people have the knack of presenting a character clearly and vigorously in a few words. It is a great gift. I have at last a clear picture of Mary Gerrard.'

'Mind you,' said Mrs. Bishop, 'I'm not saying a word *against* the girl! I wouldn't do such a thing—and she in her grave. But there's no doubt that she caused a lot of trouble!'

Poirot murmured:

'Where would it have ended, I wonder?'

'That's what *I* say!' said Mrs. Bishop. 'You can take it from me, Mr. Poirot, that if my dear mistress hadn't died when she did—awful as the shock was at the time, I see now that it was a Mercy in Disguise—I don't know what might have been the end of it!'

Poirot said invitingly:

'You mean?'

Mrs. Bishop said solemnly:

'I've come across it time and again. My own sister was in service where it happened. Once when old Colonel Randolph died and left every penny away from his poor wife to a hussy living at Eastbourne—and once old Mrs. Dacres—left it to the organist of the church—one of those long-haired young men—and she with married sons and daughters.'

Poirot said:

'You mean, I take it, that Mrs Welman might have left all her money to Mary Gerrard?'

'It wouldn't have surprised me!' said Mrs. Bishop. 'That's what the young woman was working up to, I've no doubt. And if I ventured to say a word, Mrs. Welman was ready to bite my head off, though I'd been with her nearly twenty years.

It's an ungrateful world, Mr. Poirot. You try to do your duty and it is not appreciated.'

'Alas,' sighed Poirot, 'how true that is!'

'But Wickedness doesn't always flourish,' said Mrs. Bishop.

Poirot said:

'True. Mary Gerrard is dead. . . .'

Mrs. Bishop said comfortably:

'She's gone to her reckoning, and we mustn't judge her.'

Poirot mused:

'The circumstances of her death seem quite inexplicable.'

'These police and their new-fangled ideas,' said Mrs. Bishop. 'Is it likely that a well-bred, nicely brought-up young lady like Miss Elinor would go about poisoning anyone? Trying to drag *me* into it, too, saying *I* said her manner was peculiar!'

'But was it not peculiar?'

'And why shouldn't it be?' Mrs. Bishop's bust heaved with a flash of jet. 'Miss Elinor's a young lady of feelings. She was going to turn out her aunt's things—and that's always a painful business.'

Poirot nodded sympathetically.

He said:

'It would have made it much easier for her if you had accompanied her.'

'I wanted to, Mr. Poirot, but she took me up quite sharp. Oh, well, Miss Elinor was always a very proud and reserved young lady. I wish, though, that I *had* gone with her.'

Poirot murmured:

'You did not think of following her up to the house?'

Mrs. Bishop reared her head majestically.

'I don't go where I'm not wanted, Mr. Poirot.'

Poirot looked abashed. He murmured:

'Besides, you had doubtless matters of importance to attend to that morning?'

'It was a very warm day, I remember. Very sultry.' She sighed. 'I walked to the cemetery to place a few flowers on Mrs. Welman's grave, a token of respect, and I had to rest there quite a long time. Quite overcome by the heat, I was. I got home late for lunch, and my sister was quite upset when she saw the State of Heat I was in! Said I never should have done it on a day like that.'

Poirot looked at her with admiration.

He said:

'I envy you, Mrs. Bishop. It is pleasant indeed to have

nothing with which to reproach oneself after a death. Mr. Roderick Welman, I fancy, must blame himself for not going in to see his aunt that night, though naturally he could not know she was going to pass away so soon.'

'Oh, but you're quite wrong, Mr. Poirot. I can tell you that for a fact. Mr. Roddy *did* go into his aunt's room. I was just outside on the landing myself. I'd heard that nurse go off downstairs, and I thought maybe I'd better make sure the mistress wasn't needing anything, for you know what nurses are: always staying downstairs to gossip with the maids, or else worrying them to death by asking them for things. Not that Nurse Hopkins was as bad as that red-haired Irish nurse. Always chattering and making trouble, *she* was! But, as I say, I thought I'd just see everything was all right, and it was then that I saw Mr. Roddy slip into his aunt's room. I don't know whether she knew him or not; but anyway he hasn't got anything to *reproach* himself with!'

Poirot said:

'I am glad. He is of a somewhat nervous disposition.'

'Just a trifle cranky. He always has been.'

Poirot said:

'Mrs. Bishop, you are evidently a woman of great understanding. I have formed a high regard for your judgment. What do you think is the truth about the death of Mary Gerrard?'

Mrs. Bishop snorted.

'Clear enough, I should think! One of those nasty pots of paste of Abbott's. Keeps them on those shelves for months! My second cousin was took ill and nearly died once, with tinned crab!'

Poirot objected:

'But what about the morphine found in the body?'

Mrs. Bishop said grandly:

'*I* don't know anything about morphine! I know what *doctors* are: Tell them to look for something, and they'll find it! Tainted fish paste isn't *good* enough for *them*!'

Poirot said:

'You do not think it possible that she committed suicide?'

'She?' Mrs. Bishop snorted. 'No indeed. Hadn't she made up her mind to marry Mr. Roddy? Catch *her* committing suicide!'

CHAPTER FIVE

Since it was a Sunday, Hercule Poirot found Ted Bigland at his father's farm.

There was little difficulty in getting Ted Bigland to talk. He seemed to welcome the opportunity—as though it was a relief.

He said thoughtfully:

'So you're trying to find out who killed Mary? It's a black mystery, that.'

Poirot said:

'You do not believe that Miss Carlisle killed her, then?'

Ted Bigland frowned—a puzzled, almost childlike frown it was.

He said slowly:

'Miss Elinor's a lady. She's the kind—well, you couldn't imagine her doing anything like that—anything *violent*, if you know what I mean. After all, 'tisn't likely, is it, sir, that a nice young lady would go and do a thing of that kind?'

Hercule Poirot nodded in a contemplative manner.

He said:

'No, it is not likely. . . . But when it comes to jealousy——'

He paused, watching the good-looking, fair young giant before him.

Ted Bigland said:

'Jealousy? I know things happen that way; but it's usually drink and getting worked up that makes a fellow see red and run amok. Miss Elinor—a nice quiet young lady like that——'

Poirot said:

'*But Mary Gerrard died* . . . and she did not die a natural death. Have you any idea—is there anything you can tell me to help me find out—who killed Mary Gerrard?'

Slowly the other shook his head.

He said:

'It doesn't seem right. It doesn't seem *possible*, if you take my meaning, that anyone could have killed Mary. She was—she was like a flower.'

And suddenly, for a vivid minute, Hercule Poirot had a new conception of the dead girl. . . . In that halting rustic voice the
108

girl Mary lived and bloomed again. '*She was like a flower.*'

There was suddenly a poignant sense of loss, of something exquisite destroyed. . . .

In his mind phrase after phrase succeeded each other. Peter Lord's '*She was a nice kid.*' Nurse Hopkins' '*She could have gone on the films any time.*' Mrs. Bishop's venomous '*No patience with her airs and graces.*' And now last, putting to shame, laying aside those other views, the quiet wondering: '*She was like a flower.*'

Hercule Poirot said:

'But, then . . .?'

He spread out his hands in a wide, appealing foreign gesture.

Ted Bigland nodded his head. His eyes had still the dumb, glazed look of an animal in pain.

He said:

'I know, sir. I know what you say's true. She didn't die natural. But I've been wondering . . .'

He paused.

Poirot said:

'Yes?'

Ted Bigland said slowly:

'I've been wondering if in some way it couldn't have been an *accident*?'

'An accident? But what kind of an accident?'

'I know, sir. I know. It doesn't sound like sense. But I keep thinking and thinking, and it seems to me it must have been that way. Something that wasn't meant to happen or something that was all a mistake. Just—well, just an *accident*!'

He looked pleadingly at Poirot, embarrassed by his own lack of eloquence.

Poirot was silent a moment or two. He seemed to be considering. He said at last:

'It is interesting that you feel that.'

Ted Bigland said deprecatingly:

'I dare say it doesn't make sense to you, sir. I can't figure out any *how* and *why* about it. It's just a *feeling* I've got.'

Hercule Poirot said:

'Feeling is sometimes an important guide. . . . You will pardon me, I hope, if I seem to tread on painful ground, but you cared very much for Mary Gerrard, did you not?'

A little dark colour came up in the tanned face.

Ted said simply:

'Everyone knows that around here, I reckon.'

'You wanted to marry her?'

'Yes.'

'But she—was not willing?'

Ted's face darkened a little. He said, with a hint of suppressed anger:

'Mean well, people do, but they shouldn't muck up people's lives by interfering. All this schooling and going abroad! It changed Mary. I don't mean it spoilt her, or that she was stuck-up—she wasn't. But it . . . oh, it bewildered her! She didn't know where she was any more. She was—well, put it crudely—she was too good for *me*; but she still wasn't good enough for a real gentleman like Mr. Welman.'

Hercule Poirot said, watching him:

'You don't like Mr. Welman?'

Ted Bigland said with simple violence:

'Why the hell should I? Mr. Welman's all right. I've nothing against him. He's not what I call much of a *man*! I could pick him up and break him in two. He's got brains, I suppose. . . . But that's not much help to you if your car breaks down, for instance. You may know the principle that makes a car run; but it doesn't stop you from being as helpless as a baby when all that's needed is to take the mag out and give it a wipe.'

Poirot said:

'Of course, you work in a garage?'

Ted Bigland nodded.

'Henderson's, down the road.'

'You were there on the morning when—this thing happened?'

Ted Bigland said:

'Yes, testing out a car for a gentleman. A choke somewhere, and I couldn't locate it. Ran it round for a bit. Seems odd to think of now. It was a lovely day, some honey-suckle still in the hedges. . . . Mary used to like honey-suckle. We used to go picking it together before she went away abroad. . . .'

Again there was that puzzled child-like wonder on his face. Hercule Poirot was silent.

With a start Ted Bigland came out of his trance.

He said:

'Sorry, sir, forget what I said about Mr. Welman. I was sore—because of his hanging round after Mary. He ought to
110

have left her alone. She wasn't his sort—not really.'

Poirot said:

'Do you think she cared for him?'

Again Ted Bigland frowned.

'I don't—not really. But she might have done. I couldn't say.'

Poirot asked:

'Was there any other man in Mary's life? Anyone, for instance, she had met abroad?'

'I couldn't say, sir. She never mentioned anybody.'

'Any enemies—here in Maidensford?'

'You mean anyone who had it in for her?' He shook his head. 'Nobody knew her very well. But they all liked her.'

Poirot said:

'Did Mrs. Bishop, the housekeeper at Hunterbury, like her?'

Ted gave a sudden grin. He said:

'Oh, that was just spite! The old dame didn't like Mrs. Welman taking such a fancy to Mary.'

Poirot asked:

'Was Mary Gerrard happy when she was down here? Was she fond of old Mrs. Welman?'

Ted Bigland said:

'She'd have been happy enough, I dare say, if Nurse had let her alone. Nurse Hopkins, I mean. Putting ideas into her head of earning her living and going off to do massage.'

'She was fond of Mary, though?'

'Oh, yes, she was *fond* enough of her; but she's the kind who always knows what's best for everyone!'

Poirot said slowly:

'Supposing that Nurse Hopkins knows something—something, let us say, that would throw a discreditable light on Mary—do you think she would keep it to herself?'

Ted Bigland looked at him curiously.

'I don't quite get your meaning, sir?'

'Do you think that if Nurse Hopkins knew something against Mary Gerrard she would hold her tongue about it?'

Ted Bigland said:

'I doubt if that woman could hold her tongue about anything! She's the greatest gossip in the village. But if she'd hold her tongue about *anybody*, it would probably be about Mary.' He added, his curiosity getting the better of him, 'I'd like to know *why* you ask that?'

Hercule Poirot said:

111

'One has, in talking to people, a certain impression. Nurse Hopkins was, to all seeming, perfectly frank and outspoken, but I formed the impression—very strongly—that she was keeping *something* back. It is not necessarily an *important* thing. It may have no bearing on the crime. *But there is something that she knows which she has not told.* I also formed the impression that this something—whatever it is—is something definitely damaging or detrimental to the character of Mary Gerrard. . . .'

Ted shook his head helplessly.

Hercule Poirot sighed:

'Ah, well. I shall learn what it is in time.'

CHAPTER SIX

Poirot looked with interest at the long, sensitive face of Roderick Welman.

Roddy's nerves were in a pitiable condition. His hands twitched, his eyes were bloodshot, his voice was husky and irritable.

He said, looking down at the card:

'Of course, I know your name, M. Poirot. But I don't see what Dr. Lord thinks you can do in this matter! And, anyway, what business is it of *his*? He attended my aunt, but otherwise he's a complete stranger. Elinor and I had not even met him until we went down there this June. Surely it is Seddon's business to attend to all this sort of thing?'

Hercule Poirot said:

'Technically that is correct.'

Roddy went on unhappily:

'Not that Seddon gives me much confidence. He's so confoundedly gloomy.'

'It is a habit, that, of lawyers.'

'Still,' said Roddy, cheering up a little, 'we've briefed Bulmer. He's supposed to be pretty well at the top of the tree, isn't he?'

Hercule Poirot said:

'He has a reputation for leading forlorn hopes.'

Roddy winced palpably.

Poirot said:

'It does not displease you, I hope, that I should endeavour to be of assistance to Miss Elinor Carlisle?'

'No, no, of course not. But——'

'But what can I do? It is that, that you would ask?'

A quick smile flashed across Roddy's worried face—a smile so suddenly charming that Hercule Poirot understood the subtle attraction of the man.

Roddy said apologetically:

'It sounds a little rude, put like that. But, really, of course, that *is* the point. I won't beat about the bush. What *can* you do, M. Poirot?'

Poirot said:

'I can search for the truth.'

'Yes.' Roddy sounded a little doubtful.

Poirot said:

'I might discover facts that would be helpful to the accused.'

Roddy sighed.

'If you only could!'

Hercule Poirot went on:

'It is my earnest desire to be helpful. Will you assist me by telling me just exactly what you think of the whole business?'

Roddy got up and walked restlessly up and down.

'What can I say? The whole thing's so absurd—so fantastic! The mere idea of Elinor—Elinor, whom I've known since she was a child—actually doing such a melodramatic thing as poisoning someone. It's quite laughable, of course! But how on earth explain that to a jury?'

Poirot said stolidly:

'You consider it quite impossible that Miss Carlisle should have done such a thing?'

'Oh, quite! That goes without saying! Elinor's an exquisite creature—beautifully poised and balanced—no violence in her nature. She's intellectual, sensitive and altogether devoid of animal passions. But get twelve fat-headed fools in a jury-box, and God knows what they can be made to believe! After all, let's be reasonable: they're not there to judge character; they're there to sift evidence. Facts—facts—*facts*. And the facts are unfortunate!'

Hercule Poirot nodded thoughtfully.

He said:

'You are a person, Mr. Welman, of sensibility and intelligence. The facts condemn Miss Carlisle. Your knowledge of

113

her acquits her. *What, then, really happened? What can* have happened?'

Roddy spread out his hands in exasperation.

'That's the devil of it all! I suppose the nurse couldn't have done it?'

'She was never near the sandwiches—oh, I have made the inquiries very minutely—and she could not have poisoned the tea without poisoning herself as well. I have made quite sure of that. Moreover, *why* should she wish to kill Mary Gerrard?'

Roddy cried out:

'Why should *anyone* wish to kill Mary Gerrard?'

'That,' said Poirot, 'seems to be the unanswerable question in this case. *No one* wished to kill Mary Gerrard.' (He added in his own mind: '*Except Elinor Carlisle.*') 'Therefore, the next step logically would seem to be: Mary Gerrard was not killed! But that, alas, is not so. She *was* killed!'

He added, slightly melodramatically:

> '*But she is in her grave, and oh,*
> *The difference to me!*'

'I beg your pardon,' said Roddy.

Hercule Poirot explained:

'Wordsworth. I read him much. Those lines express, perhaps, what you feel?'

'I?'

Roddy looked stiff and unapproachable.

Poirot said:

'I apologise—I apologise deeply! It is so hard—to be a detective and also a *pukka sahib*. As it is so well expressed in your language, there are things that one does not say. But, alas, a detective is forced to say them! He must ask questions: about people's private affairs, about their feelings!'

Roddy said:

'Surely all this is quite unnecessary?'

Poirot said quickly and humbly:

'If I might just understand the position? Then we will pass from the unpleasant subject and not refer to it again. It is fairly widely known, Mr. Welman, that you—admired Mary Gerrard? That is, I think, true?'

Roddy got up and stood by the window. He played with the blind tassel. He said:

'Yes.'

'You fell in love with her?'

'I suppose so.'

'Ah, and you are now heart-broken by her death——'

'I—I suppose—I mean—well, really, M. Poirot——'

He turned—a nervous, irritable, sensitive creature at bay.

Hercule Poirot said:

'If you could just tell me—just show me clearly—then it would be finished with.'

Roddy Welman sat down in a chair. He did not look at the other man. He spoke in a series of jerks.

'It's very difficult to explain. Must we go into it?'

Poirot said:

'One cannot always turn aside and pass by from the unpleasantnesses of life, Mr. Welman! You say you *suppose* you cared for this girl. You are not sure, then?'

Roddy said:

'I don't know. . . . She was so lovely. Like a dream. . . . That's what it seems like now. A dream! Not real! All that— my seeing her first—my—well, my infatuation for her! A kind of madness! And now everything is finished—gone . . . as though—as though it had never happened.'

Poirot nodded his head. . . .

He said:

'Yes, I understand. . . .'

He added:

'You were not in England yourself at the time of her death?'

'No, I went abroad on July 9th and returned on August 1st. Elinor's telegram followed me about from place to place. I hurried home as soon as I got the news.'

Poirot said:

'It must have been a great shock to you. You had cared for the girl very much.'

Roddy said, and there was bitterness and exasperation in his voice:

'Why should these things happen to one? It's not as though one *wished* them to happen! It is contrary to all—to all one's ordered expectation of life!'

Hercule Poirot said:

'Ah, but life is like that! It does not permit you to arrange and order it as you will. It will not permit you to escape emotion, to live by the intellect and by reason! You cannot say, "I will feel so much and no more." Life, Mr. Welman,

115

whatever else it is, is not *reasonable*!'

Roderick Welman murmured:

'So it seems. . . .'

Poirot said:

'A spring morning, a girl's face—and the well-ordered sequence of existence is routed.'

Roddy winced and Poirot went on:

'Sometimes it is little more than that—a *face*. What did you really know of Mary Gerrard, Mr. Welman?'

Roddy said heavily:

'What did I know? So little; I see that now. She was sweet, I think, and gentle; but really, I know nothing—nothing at all. . . . That's why, I suppose, I don't miss her. . . .'

His antagonism and resentment were gone now. He spoke naturally and simply. Hercule Poirot, as he had a knack of doing, had penetrated the other's defences. Roddy seemed to feel a certain relief in unburdening himself.

He said:

'Sweet—gentle—not very clever. Sensitive, I think, and kind. She had a refinement that you would not expect to find in a girl of her class.'

'Was she the kind of girl who would make enemies unconsciously?'

Roddy shook his head vigorously.

'No, no, I can't imagine anyone disliking her—really disliking her, I mean. Spite is different.'

Poirot said quickly:

'Spite? So there was spite, you think?'

Roddy said absently:

'Must have been—to account for that letter.'

Poirot said sharply:

'What letter?'

Roddy flushed and looked annoyed. He said:

'Oh, nothing important.'

Poirot repeated:

'What letter?'

'An anonymous letter.'

He spoke reluctantly.

'When did it come? To whom was it written?'

Rather unwillingly Roddy explained.

Hercule Poirot murmured:

'It is interesting, that. Can I see it, this letter?'

'Afraid you can't. As a matter of fact, I burnt it.'

116

'Now, why did you do that, Mr. Welman?'

Roddy said rather stiffly:

'It seemed the natural thing to do at the time.'

Poirot said:

'And in consequence of this letter, you and Miss Carlisle went hurriedly down to Hunterbury?'

'We went down, yes. I don't know about *hurriedly*.'

'But you were a little uneasy, were you not? Perhaps even, a little alarmed?'

Roddy said even more stiffly:

'I won't admit that.'

Hercule Poirot cried:

'But surely that was only natural! Your inheritance—that which was promised you—was in jeopardy! Surely it is natural that you should be unquiet about the matter! Money, it is very important!'

'Not as important as you make out.'

Poirot said:

'Such unworldliness is indeed remarkable!'

Roddy flushed. He said:

'Oh, of course, the money *did* matter to us. We weren't completely indifferent to it. But our main object was to—to see my aunt and make sure she was all right.'

Poirot said:

'You went down there with Miss Carlisle. At that time your aunt had not made a will. Shorly afterwards she had another attack of her illness. She then wished to make a will, but, conveniently for Miss Carlisle, perhaps, she dies that night before that will can be made.'

'Look here, what are you hinting at?'

Roddy's face was wrathful.

Poirot answered him like a flash:

'You have told me, Mr. Welman, as regards the death of Mary Gerrard, that the motive attributed to Elinor Carlisle is absurd—that she was, emphatically, not that kind of a person. But there is now another interpretation. Elinor Carlisle had reason to fear that she might be disinherited in favour of an outsider. The letter has warned her—her aunt's broken murmurings confirm that fear. In the hall below is an attaché-case with various drugs and medical supplies. It is easy to abstract a tube of morphine. And afterwards, so I have learned, *she sits in the sick-room alone with her aunt while you and the nurses are at dinner. . . .*'

Roddy cried:

'Good God, M. Poirot, what are you suggesting now? That Elinor killed Aunt Laura? Of all the ridiculous ideas!'

Poirot said:

'But you know, do you not, that an order to exhume Mrs. Welman's body has been applied for?'

'Yes, I know. But they won't find anything!'

'Suppose they do?'

'They won't!' Roddy spoke positively.

Poirot shook his head.

'I am not so sure. And there was only *one* person, you realise, who would benefit by Mrs. Welman's dying at that moment. . . .'

Roddy sat down. His face was white and he was shaking a little. He stared at Poirot. Then he said:

'I thought—you were on *her* side. . . .'

Hercule Poirot said:

'Whatever side one is on, one must face *facts*! I think, Mr. Welman, that you have so far preferred in life to avoid facing an awkward truth whenever it is possible.'

Roddy said:

'Why harrow oneself by looking on the worst side?'

Hercule Poirot replied gravely:

'Because it is sometimes necessary . . .'

He paused a minute and then said:

'Let us face the possibility that your aunt's death may be found to be due to the administration of morphine. What then?'

Roddy shook his head helplessly.

'I don't know.'

'But you must try to *think*. Who could have given it to her? You must admit that Elinor Carlisle had the best opportunity to do so?'

'What about the nurses?'

'Either of them could have done so, certainly. But Nurse Hopkins was concerned about the disappearance of the tube at the time and mentioned it openly. There was no need for her to do so. The death certificate had been signed. Why call attention to the missing morphine if she were guilty? It will probably bring her censure for carelessness as it is, and if she poisoned Mrs. Welman it was surely idiotic to draw attention to the morphine. Besides, what could she gain by Mrs. Welman's death? Nothing. The same applies to Nurse O'Brien. She could have administered morphine, could have taken it from Nurse Hopkins' case; but, again—*why should she?*'

Roddy shook his head.

'All that's true enough.'

Poirot said:

'Then there is *yourself*.'

Roddy started like a nervous horse.

'Me?'

'Certainly. *You* could have abstracted the morphine. *You* could have given it to Mrs. Welman! You were alone with her for a short period that night. But, again, *why should you?* If she lived to make a will, it is at least probable that you would have been mentioned in it. So again, you see, there is no motive. Only two people had a motive.'

Roddy's eyes brightened.

'*Two* people?'

'Yes. One was Elinor Carlisle.'

'And the other?'

Poirot said slowly:

'The other was the writer of that anonymous letter.'

Roddy looked incredulous.

Poirot said:

'*Somebody* wrote that letter—somebody who hated Mary Gerrard or at least disliked her—somebody who was, as they say, "on your side." Somebody, that is, *who did not want Mary Gerrard to benefit at Mrs. Welman's death*. Now, have you any idea, Mr. Welman, who the writer of that letter could be?'

Roddy shook his head.

'I've no idea at all. It was an illiterate letter, misspelt, cheap-looking.'

Poirot waved a hand.

'There is nothing much to that! It might easily have been written by an educated person who chose to disguise the fact. That is why I wish you had the letter still. People who try to write in an educated manner usually give themselves away.'

Roddy said doubtfully:

'Elinor and I thought it might be one of the servants.'

'Had you any idea which of them?'

'No—no idea whatsoever.'

'Could it, do you think, have been Mrs. Bishop, the house-keeper?'

Roddy looked shocked.

'Oh, no, she's a most respectable, high-and-mighty creature. Writes beautifully involved and ornate letters with long words in them. Besides, I'm sure she would never——'

As he hesitated, Poirot cut in:

'She did not like Mary Gerrard!'

'I suppose she didn't. I never noticed anything, though.'

'But perhaps, Mr. Welman, you do not notice very much?'

Roddy said slowly:

'You don't think, M. Poirot, that my aunt could have taken that morphine herself?'

Poirot said slowly:

'It is an idea, yes.'

Roddy said:

'She hated her—her helplessness, you know. Often said she wished she could die.'

Poirot said:

'But, then, she could not have risen from her bed, gone downstairs and helped herself to the tube of morphine from the nurse's case?'

Roddy said slowly:

'No, but somebody could have got it for her.'

'Who?'

'Well, one of the nurses.'

'No, neither of the nurses. They would understand the danger to themselves far too well! The nurses are the last people to suspect.'

'Then—somebody else . . .'

He started, opened his mouth, shut it again.

Poirot said quietly:

'You have remembered something, have you not?'

Roddy said doubtfully:

'Yes—but——'

'You wonder if you ought to tell me?'

'Well, yes . . .'

Poirot said, a curious smile tilting the corners of his mouth:

'When did Miss Carlisle say it?'

Roddy drew a deep breath.

'By Jove, you are a wizard! It was in the train coming down. We'd had the telegram, you know, saying Aunt Laura had had another stroke. Elinor said how terribly sorry she was for her, how the poor dear hated being ill, and that now she would be more helpless still and that it would be absolute hell for her. Elinor said, "One does feel that people *ought* to be set free if they themselves really want it." '

'And you said—what?'

'I agreed.'

Poirot spoke very gravely:

'Just now, Mr. Welman, you scouted the possibility of Miss Carlisle having killed your aunt for monetary gain. Do you also scout the possibility that she may have killed Mrs. Welman *out of compassion*?'

Roddy said:

'I—I—no, I can't . . .'

Hercule Poirot bowed his head.

He said:

'Yes, I thought—I was sure—that you would say that. . . . .'

CHAPTER SEVEN

In the offices of Messrs. Seddon, Blatherwick & Seddon, Hercule Poirot was received with extreme caution, not to say distrust.

Mr. Seddon, a forefinger stroking his closely shaven chin, was non-committal and his shrewd grey eyes appraised the detective thoughtfully.

'You name is familiar to me, M. Poirot, of course. But I am at a loss to understand your position in this case.'

Hercule Poirot said:

'I am acting, Monsieur, in the interests of your client.'

'Ah—indeed? And who—er—engaged you in that capacity?'

'I am here at the request of Dr. Lord.'

Mr. Seddon's eyebrows rose very high.

'Indeed! That seems to me very irregular—very irregular. Dr. Lord, I understand, has been subpœnaed as a witness for the prosecution.'

Hercule Poirot shrugged his shoulders.

'Does that matter?'

Mr. Seddon said:

'The arrangements for Miss Carlisle's defence are entirely in our hands. I really do not think we need any outside assistance in this case.'

Poirot asked:

'Is that because your client's innocence will be so easily proved?'

Mr. Seddon winced. Then he became wrathful in a dry legal fashion.

'That,' he said, 'is a most improper question. Most improper.'

Hercule Poirot said:

'The case against your client is a very strong one. . . .'

'I really fail to see, M. Poirot, how you know anything about it.'

Poirot said:

'Although I am actually retained by Dr. Lord, I have here a note from Mr. Roderick Welman.'

He handed it over with a bow.

Mr. Seddon perused the few lines it contained and remarked grudgingly:

'That, of course, throws a new complexion on the matter. Mr. Welman has made himself responsible for Miss Carlisle's defence. We are acting at his request.'

He added with visible distaste:

'Our firm does very little in—er—criminal procedure, but I felt it my duty to my—er—late client—to undertake the defence of her niece. I may say we have already briefed Sir Edwin Bulmer, K.C.'

Poirot said, and his smile was suddenly ironic:

'No expense will be spared. Very right and proper!'

Looking over his glasses, Mr. Seddon said:

'Really, M. Poirot——'

Poirot cut into his protest.

'Eloquence and emotional appeal will not save your client. It will need more than that.'

Mr. Seddon said dryly:

'What do you advise?'

'There is always the truth.'

'Quite so.'

'But in this case will the truth help us?'

Mr. Seddon said sharply:

'That, again, is a most improper remark.'

Poirot said:

'There are certain questions to which I should like answers.'

Mr. Seddon said cautiously:

'I cannot, of course, guarantee to answer without the consent of my client.'

'Naturally. I understand that.' He paused and then said, 'Has Elinor Carlisle any enemies?'

Mr. Seddon showed a faint surprise.

'As far as I know, none.'

'Did the late Mrs. Welman, at any period of her life, make a will?'

'Never. She always put it off.'

'Has Elinor Carlisle made a will?'

'Yes.'

'Recently? Since her aunt's death?'

'Yes.'

'To whom has she left her property?'

'That, M. Poirot, is confidential. I cannot tell you without authorisation from my client.'

Poirot said:

'Then I shall have to interview your client!'

Mr. Seddon said with a cold smile:

'That, I fear, will not be easy.'

Poirot rose and made a gesture.

'Everything,' he said, 'is easy to Hercule Poirot.'

CHAPTER EIGHT

Chief Inspector Marsden was affable.

'Well, M. Poirot,' he said. 'Come to set me right about one of my cases?'

Poirot murmured deprecatingly:

'No, no. A little curiosity on my part, that is all.'

'Only too happy to satisfy it. Which case is it?'

'Elinor Carlisle.'

'Oh, yes, girl who poisoned Mary Gerrard. Coming up for trial in two weeks' time. Interesting case. She did in the old woman too, by the way. Final report isn't in yet, but it seems there's no doubt of it. Morphia. Cold-blooded bit of goods. Never turned a hair at the time of her arrest or after. Giving nothing away. But we've got the goods on her all right. She's for it.'

'You think she did it?'

123

Marsden, an experienced, kindly looking man, nodded his head affirmatively.

'Not a doubt of it. Put the stuff in the top sandwich. She's a cool customer.'

'You have no doubts? No doubts at all?'

'Oh, no! I'm quite sure. It's a pleasant feeling when you *are* sure! We don't like making mistakes any more than anyone else would. We're not just out to get a conviction, as some people think. This time I can go ahead with a clear conscience.'

Poirot said slowly:

'I see.'

The Scotland Yard man looked at him curiously.

'Is there anything on the other side?'

Slowly Poirot shook his head.

'As yet, no. So far everything I have found out about the case points to Elinor Carlisle's being guilty.'

Inspector Marsden said with cheerful certainty:

'*She's* guilty, all right.'

Poirot said:

'I should like to see her.'

Inspector Marsden smiled indulgently. He said:

'Got the present Home Secretary in your pocket, haven't you? That will be easy enough.'

CHAPTER NINE

Peter Lord said:

'Well?'

Hercule Poirot said:

'No, it is not very well.'

Peter Lord said heavily:

'You haven't got hold of anything?'

Poirot said slowly:

'Elinor Carlisle killed Mary Gerrard out of jealousy. . . . Elinor Carlisle killed her aunt so as to inherit her money. . . . Elinor Carlisle killed her aunt out of compassion. . . . My friend, you may make your choice!'

Peter Lord said:

'You're talking nonsense!'

Hercule Poirot said:

'Am I?'

Lord's freckled face looked angry. He said:

'What *is* all this?'

Hercule Poirot said:

'Do you think it is possible, that?'

'Do I think what is possible?'

'That Elinor Carlisle was unable to bear the sight of her aunt's misery and helped her out of existence.'

'Nonsense!'

'Is it nonsense? You have told me yourself that the old lady asked *you* to help her.'

'She didn't mean it seriously. She knew I wouldn't do anything of the sort.'

'Still, the idea was in her mind. Elinor Carlisle *might* have helped her.'

Peter Lord strolled up and down. He said at last:

'One can't deny that that sort of thing is possible. But Elinor Carlisle is a level-headed, clear-thinking kind of young woman. I don't think she'd be so carried away by pity as to lose sight of the risk. And she'd realise exactly what the risk was. She'd be liable to stand accused of murder.'

'So you don't think she would do it?'

Peter Lord said slowly:

'I think a woman might do such a thing for her husband; or for her child; or for her mother, perhaps. I don't think she'd do it for an aunt, though she might be fond of that aunt. And I think in any case she'd only do it if the person in question was actually suffering unbearable pain.'

Poirot said thoughtfully:

'Perhaps you are right.'

Then he added:

'Do you think Roderick Welman's feelings could have been sufficiently worked upon to induce *him* to do such a thing?'

Peter Lord replied scornfully:

'He wouldn't have the guts!'

Poirot murmured:

'I wonder. In some ways, *mon cher*, you underestimate that young man.'

'Oh, he's clever and intellectual and all that, I dare say.'

'Exactly,' said Poirot. 'And he has charm, too. . . , Yes, I felt that.'

'Did you? I never have!'

Then Peter Lord said earnestly:

'Look here, Poirot, isn't there *anything*?'

Poirot said:

'They are not fortunate so far, my investigations! They lead always back to the same place. No one stood to gain by Mary Gerrard's death. No one hated Mary Gerrard—*except* Elinor Carlisle. There is only one question that we might perhaps ask ourselves. We might say, perhaps: *Did anyone hate Elinor Carlisle?*'

Slowly Dr. Lord shook his head.

'Not that I know of. . . . You mean—that someone might have framed her for the crime?'

Poirot nodded. He said:

'It is a very far-fetched speculation, that, and there is nothing to support it . . . except, perhaps, the very completeness of the case against her.'

He told the other of the anonymous letter.

'You see,' he said, 'that makes it possible to outline a very strong case against her. She was warned that she might be completely cut out of her aunt's will—that this girl, a stranger, might get all the money. So, when her aunt in her halting speech was asking for a lawyer, Elinor took no chances, and saw to it that the old lady should die that night!'

Peter Lord cried:

'What about Roderick Welman? He stood to lose, too!'

Poirot shook his head.

'No, it was to his advantage that the old lady should make a will. If she died intestate, he got nothing, remember. Elinor was the next of kin.'

Lord said:

'But he was going to marry Elinor!'

Poirot said, 'True. But remember that immediately afterwards the engagement was broken off—that he showed her clearly that he wished to be released from it.'

Peter Lord groaned and held his head. He said:

'It comes back to her, then. Every time!'

'Yes. Unless . . .'

He was silent for a minute. Then he said:

'There is *something* . . .'

'Yes?'

'Something—some little piece of the puzzle that is missing. It is something—of that I am certain—that concerns Mary Gerrard. My friend, you hear a certain amount of gossip, of scandal, down here. Have you ever heard anything against her?'

'Against Mary Gerrard? Her character, you mean?'

'Anything. Some bygone story about her. Some indiscretion on her part. A hint of scandal. A doubt of her honesty. A malicious rumour concerning her. Anything—anything at all— but something that definitely is *damaging to her. . . .*'

Peter Lord said slowly:

'I hope you're not going to suggest that line. . . . Trying to rake up things about a harmless young woman who's dead and can't defend herself. . . . And, anyway, I don't believe you can do it!'

'She was like the female Sir Galahad—a blameless life?'

'As far as I know, she was. I never heard anything else.'

Poirot said gently:

'You must not think, my friend, that I would stir the mud where no mud is. . . . No, no, it is not like that at all. But the good Nurse Hopkins is not an adept at hiding her feelings. She was fond of Mary, and there is something about Mary she does not want known; that is to say, there is something against Mary that she is afraid I will find out. She does not think that it has any bearing on the crime. But, then, she is convinced that the crime was committed by Elinor Carlisle, and clearly this fact, whatever it is, has nothing to do with Elinor. But, you see, my friend, it is imperative that I should know *everything*. For it may be that there is a wrong done by Mary to some third person, and in that case, that third person might have a motive for desiring her death.'

Peter Lord said:

'But surely, in that case, Nurse Hopkins would realise that, too.'

Poirot said:

'Nurse Hopkins is quite an intelligent woman within her limitations, but her intellect is hardly the equal of *mine. She* might not see, but Hercule Poirot would!'

Peter Lord said, shaking his head:

'I'm sorry. I don't know anything.'

Poirot said thoughtfully:

'No more does Ted Bigland—and he has lived here all his life and Mary's. No more does Mrs. Bishop; for if she knew anything unpleasant about the girl, she would not have been able to keep it to herself! *Eh bien*, there is one more hope.'

'Yes?'

'I am seeing the other nurse, Nurse O'Brien, to-day.'

Peter Lord said, shaking his head:

'She doesn't know much about this part of the world. She was only here for a month or two.'

Poirot said:

'I am aware of that. But, my friend, Nurse Hopkins, we have been told, has the long tongue. She has not gossiped in the village, where such talk might have done Mary Gerrard harm. But I doubt if she could refrain from giving at least a hint about something that was occupying her mind to a stranger and a colleague! Nurse O'Brien *may* know something.'

CHAPTER TEN

Nurse O'Brien tossed her red head and smiled widely across the tea-table at the little man opposite her.

She thought to herself:

'It's the funny little fellow he is—and his eyes green like any cat's, and with all that Dr. Lord saying he's the clever one!'

Hercule Poirot said:

'It is a pleasure to meet someone so full of health and vitality. Your patients, I am sure, must all recover.'

Nurse O'Brien said:

'I'm not one for pulling a long face, and not many of my patients die on me, I'm thankful to say.'

Poirot said:

'Of course, in Mrs. Welman's case, it was a merciful release.'

'Ah! It was that, the poor dear.' Her eyes were shrewd as she looked at Poirot and asked:

'Is it about that you want to talk to me? I was after hearing that they're digging her up.'

Poirot said:

'You yourself had no suspicion at the time?'

'Not the least in the world, though indeed I might have had, with the face Dr. Lord had on him that morning, and him sending me here, there and everywhere for things he didn't need! But he signed the certificate, for all that.'

Poirot began, 'He had his reasons——' but she took the words out of his mouth.

'Indeed and he was right. It does a doctor no good to think things and offend the family, and then if he's wrong it's the end of him, and no one would be wishing to call him in any more. A doctor's got to be *sure*!'

Poirot said:

'There is a suggestion that Mrs. Welman might have committed suicide.'

'She? And her lying there helpless? Just lift one hand, that was all *she* could do!'

'Someone might have helped her?'

'Ah! I see now what you're meaning. Miss Carlisle, or Mr. Welman, or maybe Mary Gerrard?'

'It would be possible, would it not?'

Nurse O'Brien shook her head. She said:

'They'd not dare—any of them!'

Poirot said slowly:

'Perhaps not.'

Then he said:

'When was it Nurse Hopkins missed the tube of morphine?'

'It was that very morning. "I'm sure I had it here," she said. Very sure she was at first; but you know how it is, after a while your mind gets confused, and in the end she made sure she'd left it at home.'

Poirot murmured:

'And even then you had no suspicion?'

'Not the least in the world! Sure, it never entered my head for a moment that things weren't as they should be. And even now 'tis only a suspicion they have.'

'The thought of that missing tube never caused either you or Nurse Hopkins an uneasy moment?'

'Well, I wouldn't say that. . . . I do remember that it came into my head—and into Nurse Hopkins' head, too, I believe —in the Blue Tit Café, we were at the time. And I saw the thought pass into her mind from mine. "It couldn't be any other way than that I left it on the mantelpiece and it fell into the dustbin, could it?" she says. And "No, indeed, that was the way of it," I said to her; and neither of us saying what was in our minds and the fear that was on us.'

Hercule Poirot asked:

'And what do you think now?'

Nurse O'Brien said:

S.C.—E

'If they find morphine in her there'll be little doubt who took that tube, nor what it was used for—though I'll not be believing she sent the old lady the same road till it's proved there's morphine in her.'

Poirot said:

'You have no doubt at all that Elinor Carlisle killed Mary Gerrard?'

'There's no question of it at all, in my opinion! Who else had the reason or the wish to do it?'

'That is the question,' said Poirot.

Nurse O'Brien went on dramatically:

'Wasn't I there that night when the old lady was trying to speak, and Miss Elinor promising her that everything should be done decently and according to her wishes? And didn't I see her face looking after Mary as she went down the stairs one day, and the black hate that was on it? 'Twas murder she had in her heart that minute.'

Poirot said:

'If Elinor Carlisle killed Mrs. Welman, why did she do it?'

'Why? For the money, of course. Two hundred thousand pounds, no less. That's what she got by it, and that's why she did it—if she did it. She's a bold, clever young lady, with no fear in her, and plenty of brains.'

Hercule Poirot said:

'If Mrs. Welman had lived to make a will, how do you think she'd have left her money?'

'Ah, it's not for me to be saying that,' said Nurse O'Brien, betraying, however, every symptom of being about to do so. 'But it's my opinion that every penny the old lady had would have gone to Mary Gerrard.'

'Why?' said Hercule Poirot.

The simple monosyllable seemed to upset Nurse O'Brien.

'Why? Is it *why* you're asking? Well—I'd say that that would be the way of it.'

Poirot murmured:

'Some people might say that Mary Gerrard had played her cards very cleverly, that she had managed so to ingratiate herself with the old woman, as to make her forget the ties of blood and affection.'

'They might that,' said Nurse O'Brien slowly.

Poirot asked:

'*Was* Mary Gerrard a clever, scheming girl?'

Nurse O'Brien said, still rather slowly:

'I'll not think that of her. . . . All she did was natural enough, with no thought of scheming. She wasn't that kind. And there's reasons often for these things that never get made public. . . .'

Hercule Poirot said softly:

'You are, I think, a very discreet woman, Nurse O'Brien.'

'I'm not one to be talking of what doesn't concern me.'

Watching her very closely, Poirot went on:

'You and Nurse Hopkins, you have agreed together, have you not, that there are some things which are best not brought out into the light of day.'

Nurse O'Brien said:

'What would you be meaning by that?'

Poirot said quickly:

'Nothing to do with the crime—or crimes. I mean—the other matter.'

Nurse O'Brien said, nodding her head:

'What would be the use of raking up mud and an old story, and she a decent elderly woman with never a breath of scandal about her, and dying respected and looked up to by everybody.'

Hercule Poirot nodded in assent. He said cautiously:

'As you say, Mrs. Welman was much respected in Maidensford.'

The conversation had taken an unexpected turn, but his face expressed no surprise or puzzlement.

Nurse O'Brien went on:

'It's so long ago, too. All dead and forgotten. I've a soft heart for a romance myself, and I do say and I always have said that it's hard for a man who's got a wife in an asylum to be tied all his life with nothing but death that can free him.'

Poirot murmured, still in bewilderment:

'Yes, it is hard . . .'

Nurse O'Brien said:

'Did Nurse Hopkins tell you how her letter crossed mine?'

Poirot said truthfully:

'She did not tell me *that*.'

' 'Twas an odd coincidence. But there, that's always the way of it! Once you hear a name, maybe, and a day or two later you'll come across it again, and so on and so on. That I should be seeing the self-same photograph on the piano and at the same minute Nurse Hopkins was hearing all about it from the doctor's housekeeper.'

'That,' said Poirot, 'is very interesting.'

He murmured tentatively:

'Did Mary Gerrard know—about this?'

'Who'd be telling her?' said Nurse O'Brien. 'Not I—and not Hopkins. After all, what good would it be to her?'

She flung up her red head and gazed at him steadily.

Poirot said with a sigh:

'What, indeed?'

CHAPTER ELEVEN

Elinor Carlisle : : :

Across the width of the table that separated them Poirot looked at her searchingly.

They were alone together. Through a glass wall a warder watched them.

Poirot noted the sensitive intelligent face with the square, white forehead, and the delicate modelling of the ears and nose. Fine lines; a proud, sensitive creature, showing breeding, self-restraint and—something else—a capacity for passion.

He said:

'I am Hercule Poirot. I have been sent to you by Dr. Peter Lord. He thinks that I can help you.'

Elinor Carlisle said:

'Peter Lord. . . .' Her tone was reminiscent. For a moment she smiled a little wistfully. She went on formally: 'It was kind of him, but I do not think there is anything you can do.'

Hercule Poirot said:

'Will you answer my questions?'

She sighed. She said:

'Believe me—really—it would be better not to ask them. I am in good hands. Mr. Seddon has been most kind. I am to have a very famous counsel.'

Poirot said:

'He is not so famous as I am!'

Elinor Carlisle said with a touch of weariness:

'He has a great reputation.'

'Yes, for defending criminals. I have a great reputation—for demonstrating innocence.'

She lifted her eyes at last—eyes of a vivid, beautiful blue. They looked straight into Poirot's. She said:

'Do you believe I am innocent?'

Hercule Poirot said:

'Are you?'

Elinor smiled, an ironic little smile. She said:

'Is that a sample of your questions? It is very easy, isn't it, to answer Yes?'

He said unexpectedly:

'You are very tired, are you not?'

Her eyes widened a little. She answered:

'Why, yes—that more than anything. How did you know?'

Hercule Poirot said:

'I knew . . .'

Elinor said:

'I shall be glad when it is—over.'

Poirot looked at her for a minute in silence. Then he said:

'I have seen your—cousin, shall I call him for convenience?—Mr. Roderick Welman.'

Into the white proud face the colour crept slowly up. He knew then that one question of his was answered without his asking it.

She said, and her voice shook very slightly:

'You've seen Roddy?'

Poirot said:

'He is doing all he can for you.'

'I know.'

Her voice was quick and soft.

Poirot said:

'Is he poor or rich?'

'Roddy? He has not very much money of his own.'

'And he is extravagant?'

She said, almost absently:

'Neither of us ever thought it mattered. We knew that some day . . .'

She stopped.

Poirot said quickly:

'You counted on your inheritance? That is understandable.'

He went on:

'You have heard, perhaps, the result of the autopsy on your aunt's body. She died of morphine poisoning.'

Elinor Carlisle said coldly:

'I did not kill her.'

'Did you help her to kill herself?'

'Did I help——? Oh, I see. No, I did not.'

'Did you know that your aunt had not made a will?'

'No, I had no idea of that.'

Her voice was flat now—dull. The answer was mechanical, uninterested.

Poirot said:

'And you yourself, have you made a will?'

'Yes.'

'Did you make it the day Dr. Lord spoke to you about it?'

'Yes.'

Again that swift wave of colour.

Poirot said:

'How have you left your fortune, Miss Carlisle?'

Elinor said quietly:

'I have left everything to Roddy—to Roderick Welman.'

Poirot said:

'Does he know that?'

She said quickly:

'Certainly not.'

'You didn't discuss it with him?'

'Of course not. He would have been horribly embarrassed and would have disliked what I was doing very much.'

'Who else knows the contents of your will?'

'Only Mr. Seddon—and his clerks, I suppose.'

'Did Mr. Seddon draw up the will for you?'

'Yes. I wrote to him that same evening—I mean the evening of the day Dr. Lord spoke to me about it.'

'Did you post your letter yourself?'

'No. It went in the box from the house with the other letters.'

'You wrote it, put it in an envelope, sealed it, stamped it and put it in the box—*comme ça*? You did not pause to reflect? To read it over?'

Elinor said, staring at him:

'I read it over—yes. I had gone to look for some stamps. When I came back with them, I just re-read the letter to be sure I had put it clearly.'

'Was anyone in the room with you?'

'Only Roddy.'

'Did he know what you were doing?'

'I told you—no.'

'Could anyone have read that letter when you were out of the room?'

'I don't know. . . . One of the servants, you mean? I suppose they could have if they had chanced to come in while I was out of the room.'

'And before Mr. Roderick Welman entered it?'

'Yes.'

Poirot said:

'And he could have read it, too?'

Elinor's voice was clear and scornful. She said:

'I can assure you, M. Poirot, that my "cousin," as you call him, does not read other people's letters.'

Poirot said:

'That is the accepted idea, I know. You would be surprised how many people do the things that "are not done." '

Elinor shrugged her shoulders.

Poirot said in a casual voice:

'Was it on that day that the idea of killing Mary Gerrard first came to you?'

For the third time colour swept over Elinor Carlisle's face. This time it was a burning tide. She said:

'Did Peter Lord tell you that?'

Poirot said gently:

'It *was* then, wasn't it? When you looked through the window and saw her making her will. It was then, was it not, that it struck you how funny it would be—and how convenient—if Mary Gerrard should happen to die. . . .'

Elinor said in a low suffocated voice:

'He knew—he looked at me and he knew . . .'

Poirot said:

'Dr. Lord knows a good deal. . . . He is no fool, that young man with the freckled face and the red hair. . . .'

Elinor said in a low voice:

'Is it true that he sent you to—help me?'

'It is true, Mademoiselle.'

She sighed and said:

'I don't understand. No, I don't understand.'

Poirot said:

'Listen, Miss Carlisle. It is necessary that you tell me just what happened that day when Mary Gerrard died: where you went, what you did; more than that, I want to know even what you thought.'

She stared at him. Then slowly a queer little smile came to her lips. She said:

'You must be an incredibly simple man. Don't you realise how easy it is for me to lie to you?'

Hercule Poirot said placidly:

'It does not matter.'

She was puzzled.

'Not matter?'

'No. For lies, Mademoiselle, tell a listener just as much as truth can. Sometimes they tell more. Come, now, commence. You met your housekeeper, the good Mrs. Bishop. She wanted to come and help you. You would not let her. Why?'

'I wanted to be alone.'

'Why?'

'Why? Why? Because I wanted to—to think.'

'You wanted to imagine—yes. And then what did you do next?'

Elinor, her chin raised defiantly, said:

'I bought some paste for sandwiches.'

'Two pots?'

'Two.'

'And you went to Hunterbury. What did you do there?'

'I went up to my aunt's room and began to go through her things.'

'What did you find?'

'Find?' She frowned. 'Clothes—old letters—photographs—jewellery.'

Poirot said:

'No secrets?'

'Secrets? I don't understand you.'

'Then let us proceed. What next?'

Elinor said:

'I came down to the pantry and I cut sandwiches. . . .'

Poirot said softly:

'And you thought—what?'

Her blue eyes flashed suddenly. She said:

'I thought of my namesake, Eleanor of Aquitaine . . .'

Poirot said:

'I understand perfectly.'

'Do you?'

'Oh, yes. I know the story. She offered Fair Rosamund, did she not, the choice of a dagger *or a cup of poison*. Rosamund chose the poison . . .'

Elinor said nothing. She was white now.

Poirot said:

'But perhaps, this time, *there was to be no choice. . . .* Go on, Mademoiselle, what next?'

Elinor said:

'I put the sandwiches ready on a plate and I went down to the Lodge. Nurse Hopkins was there as well as Mary. I told them I had some sandwiches up at the house.'

Poirot was watching her. He said softly:

'Yes, and you all came up to the house together, did you not?'

'Yes. We—ate the sandwiches in the morning-room.'

Poirot said in the same soft tone:

'Yes, yes—*still in the dream. . . .* And then . . .'

'Then?' She stared. 'I left her—standing by the window. I went out into the pantry. It was still like you say—*in a dream.* . . . Nurse was there washing up. . . . I gave her the paste-pot.'

'Yes—yes. And what happened then? What did you think of next?'

Elinor said dreamily:

'There was a mark on Nurse's wrist. I mentioned it and she said it was a thorn from the rose trellis by the Lodge. *The roses by the Lodge.* . . . Roddy and I had a quarrel once—long ago —about the Wars of the Roses. I was Lancaster and he was York. He liked white roses. I said they weren't real—they didn't even smell! I liked red roses, big and dark and velvety and smelling of summer. . . . We quarrelled in the most idiotic way. You see, it all came back to me—there in the pantry— and something—something broke—the black hate I'd had in my heart—it went away—with remembering how we were together as children. I didn't hate Mary any more. I didn't want her to die . . .'

She stopped.

'But later, when we went back into the morning-room, she was dying. . . .'

She stopped. Poirot was staring at her very intently. She flushed and said:

'Will you ask me—again—*did I kill Mary Gerrard?*'

Poirot rose to his feet. He said quickly:

'I shall ask you—nothing. There are things I do not want to know. . . .'

CHAPTER TWELVE

I

Dr. Lord met the train at the station as requested.

Hercule Poirot alighted from it. He looked very Londonified and was wearing pointed patent leather shoes.

Peter Lord scrutinised his face anxiously, but Hercule Poirot was giving nothing away.

Peter Lord said:

'I've done my best to get answers to your questions. First, Mary Gerrard left here for London on July 10th. Second, I haven't got a housekeeper—a couple of giggling girls run my house. I think you must mean Mrs. Slattery, who was Ransome's (my predecessor's) housekeeper. I can take you to her this morning if you like. I've arranged that she shall be in.'

Poirot said:

'Yes, I think it would be as well if I saw her first.'

'Then you said you wanted to go to Hunterbury, I could come with you there. It beats me why you haven't been there already. I can't think why you wouldn't go when you were down here before. I should have thought the first thing to be done in a case like this was to visit the place where the crime took place.'

Holding his head a little on one side, Hercule Poirot inquired:

'Why?'

'Why?' Peter Lord was rather disconcerted by the question. 'Isn't it the usual thing to do?'

Hercule Poirot said:

'One does not practise detection with a textbook! One uses one's natural intelligence.'

Peter Lord said:

'You might find a clue of some sort there.'

Poirot sighed:

'You read too much detective fiction. Your police force in this country is quite admirable. I have no doubt that they searched the house and grounds most carefully.'

'For evidence *against* Elinor Carlisle—not for evidence in her favour.'

Poirot sighed:

'My dear friend, it is not a monster—this police force! Elinor Carlisle was arrested because sufficient evidence was found to make out a case against her—a very strong case, I may say. It was useless for me to go over ground when the police had gone over it already.'

'But you do want to go there now?' objected Peter.

Hercule Poirot nodded his head.

He said:

'Yes—now it is necessary. Because now I know *exactly what I am looking for*. One must understand with the cells of one's brain before one uses one's eyes.'

'Then you *do* think there might be—something—there still?'

Poirot said gently:

'I have a little idea we shall find something—yes.'

'Something to prove Elinor's innocence?'

'Ah, I did not say that.'

Peter Lord stopped dead.

'You don't mean you *still* think she's guilty?'

Poirot said gravely:

'You must wait, my friend, before you get an answer to that question.'

II

Poirot lunched with the doctor in a pleasant square room with a window open on to the garden.

Lord said:

'Did you get what you wanted out of old Slattery?'

Poirot nodded.

'Yes.'

'What *did* you want with her?'

'Gossip! Talk about old days. Some crimes have their roots in the past. I think this one had.'

Peter Lord said irritably:

'I don't understand a word you are talking about.'

Poirot smiled. He said:

'This fish is deliciously fresh.'

Lord said impatiently:

'I dare say. I caught it myself before breakfast this morning. Look here, Poirot, am I to have any idea what you're driving at? Why keep me in the dark?'

The other shook his head.

'Because as yet there is no light. I am always brought up short by the fact that there was no one who had any reason to kill Mary Gerrard—except Elinor Carlisle.'

Peter Lord said:

'You can't be sure of that. She'd been abroad for some time, remember.'

'Yes, yes, I have made the inquiries.'

'You've been to Germany yourself?'

'Myself, no.' With a slight chuckle he added: 'I have my spies!'

'Can you depend on other people?'

'Certainly. It is not for me to run here and there, doing amateurishly the things that for a small sum someone else can do with professional skill. I can assure you, *mon cher*, I have several irons on the fire. I have some useful assistants—one of them a former burglar.'

'What do you use him for?'

'The last thing I have used him for was a very thorough search of Mr. Welman's flat.'

'What was he looking for?'

Poirot said:

'One always likes to know exactly what lies have been told one.'

'Did Welman tell you a lie?'

'Definitely.'

'Who else has lied to you?'

'Everybody, I think: Nurse O'Brien romantically; Nurse Hopkins stubbornly; Mrs. Bishop venomously. You yourself——'

'Good God!' Peter Lord interrupted him unceremoniously. 'You don't think I've lied to you, do you?'

'Not yet,' Poirot admitted.

Dr. Lord sank back in his chair. He said:

'You're a disbelieving sort of fellow, Poirot.'

Then he said:

'If you've finished, shall we set off for Hunterbury? I've got some patients to see later, and then there's the surgery.'

'I am at your disposal, my friend.'

They set off on foot, entering the grounds by the back drive. Half-way up it they met a tall, good-looking young fellow wheeling a barrow. He touched his cap respectfully to Dr. Lord.

'Good-morning, Horlick. This is Horlick, the gardener, Poirot. He was working here that morning.'

Horlick said:

'Yes, sir, I was. I saw Miss Elinor that morning and talked to her.'

Poirot asked:

'What did she say to you?'

'She told me the house was as good as sold, and that rather took me aback, sir; but Miss Elinor said as how she'd speak for me to Major Somervell, and that maybe he'd keep me on —if he didn't think me too young, perhaps, as head—seeing as how I'd had good training under Mr. Stephens, here.'

Dr. Lord said:

'Did she seem much the same as usual, Horlick?'

'Why, yes, sir, except that she looked a bit excited like— and as though she had something on her mind.'

Hercule Poirot said:

'Did you know Mary Gerrard?'

'Oh, yes, sir. But not very well.'

Poirot said:

'What was she like?'

Horlick looked puzzled.

'Like, sir? Do you mean to look at?'

'Not exactly. I mean, what kind of a girl was she?'

'Oh, well, sir, she was a very superior sort of a girl. Nice spoken and all that. Thought a lot of herself, I should say. You see, old Mrs. Welman had made a lot of fuss over her. Made her father wild, that did. He was like a bear with a sore head about it.'

Poirot said:

'By all that I've heard, he had not the best of tempers, that old one?'

'No, indeed, he hadn't. Always grumbling, and crusty as they make them. Seldom had a civil word for you.'

Poirot said:

'You were here on that morning. Whereabouts were you working?'

'Mostly in the kitchen garden, sir.'

'You cannot see the house from there?'

'No, sir.'

Peter Lord said:

'If anybody had come up to the house—up to the pantry window—you wouldn't have seen them?'

'No, I wouldn't, sir.'

Peter Lord said:

'When did you go to your dinner?'

'One o'clock, sir.'

'And you didn't see anything—any man hanging about—or a car outside—anything like that?'

The man's eyebrows rose in slight surprise.

'Outside the back gate, sir? There was your car there—nobody else's.'

Peter Lord cried:

'*My* car? It wasn't my car! I was over Withenbury direction that morning. Didn't get back till after two.'

Horlick looked puzzled.

'I made sure it was your car, sir,' he said doubtfully.

Peter Lord said quickly:

'Oh, well, it doesn't matter. Good-morning, Horlick.'

He and Poirot moved on. Horlick stared after them for a minute or two, then slowly resumed his progress with the wheelbarrow.

Peter Lord said softly—but with great excitement:

'Something—at last. Whose car was it standing in the lane that morning?'

Poirot said:

'What make is your car, my friend?'

'A Ford ten—sea-green. They're pretty common, of course.'

'And you are sure that it was not yours? You haven't mistaken the day?'

'Absolutely certain. I was over at Withebury, came back late, snatched a bit of lunch, and then the call came through about Mary Gerrard and I rushed over.'

Poirot said softly:

'Then it would seem, my friend, that we have come upon something tangible at last.'

Peter Lord said:

'*Someone was here that morning* . . . someone who was not Elinor Carlisle, nor Mary Gerrard, nor Nurse Hopkins . . .'

Poirot said:

'This is very interesting. Come, let us make our investigations. Let us see, for instance, supposing a man (or woman) were to wish to approach the house unseen, how they would set about it.'

Half-way along the drive a path branched off through some shrubbery. They took this and at a certain turn in it Peter

Lord clutched Poirot's arm, pointing to a window.

He said:

'That's the window of the pantry where Elinor Carlisle was cutting the sandwiches.'

Poirot murmured:

'And from here, *anyone could see her cutting them*. The window was open, if I remember rightly?'

Peter Lord said:

'It was wide open. It was a hot day, remember.'

Hercule Poirot said musingly:

'Then if anyone wished to watch unseen what was going on, somewhere about here would be a good spot.'

The two men cast about. Peter Lord said:

'There's a place here—behind these bushes. Some stuff's been trampled down here. It's grown up again now, but you can see plainly enough.'

Poirot joined him. He said thoughtfully:

'Yes, this is a good place. It is concealed from the path, and that opening in the shrubs gives one a good view of the window. Now, what did he do, our friend who stood here? Did he perhaps smoke?'

They bent down, examining the ground and pushing aside the leaves and branches.

Suddenly Hercule Poirot uttered a grunt.

Peter Lord straightened up from his own search.

'What is it?'

'A match-box, my friend. An empty match-box, trodden heavily into the ground, sodden and decayed.'

With care and delicacy he salved the object. He displayed it at last on a sheet of notepaper taken from his pocket.

Peter Lord said:

'It's foreign. My God! *German matches!*'

Hercule Poirot said:

'And Mary Gerrard had recently come from Germany!'

Peter Lord said exultantly:

'We've got something now! You can't deny it.'

Hercule Poirot said slowly:

'Perhaps . . .'

'But, damn it all, man. Who on earth round here would have had foreign matches?'

Hercule Poirot said:

'I know—I know.'

His eyes, perplexed eyes, went to the gap in the bushes and

the view of the window.

He said:

'It is not quite so simple as you think. There is one great difficulty. Do you not see it yourself?'

'What? Tell me.'

Poirot sighed.

'If you do not see for yourself . . . But come, let us go on.'

They went on to the house. Peter Lord unlocked the back door with a key.

He led the way through the scullery to the kitchen, through that, along a passage where there was a cloakroom on one side and the butler's pantry on the other. The two men looked round the pantry.

It had the usual cupboards with sliding glass doors for glass and china. There was a gas-ring and two kettles and canisters marked Tea and Coffee on a shelf above. There was a sink and draining-board and a papier-mâché washing-up bowl. In front of the window was a table.

Peter Lord said:

'It was on this table that Elinor Carlisle cut the sandwiches. The fragment of the morphine label was found in this crack in the floor under the sink.'

Poirot said thoughtfully:

'The police are careful searchers. They do not miss much.'

Peter Lord said violently:

'There's no evidence that Elinor ever handled that tube! I tell you, someone was watching her from the shrubbery outside. She went down to the Lodge and he saw his chance and slipped in, uncorked the tube, crushed some tablets of morphine to powder and put them into the top sandwich. He never noticed that he'd torn a bit off the label of the tube, and that it had fluttered down the crack. He hurried away, started up his car and went off again.'

Poirot sighed.

'And still you do not see! It is extraordinary how dense an intelligent man can be.'

Peter Lord demanded angrily:

'Do you mean to say that you don't believe someone stood in those bushes watching the window?'

Poirot said:

'Yes, I believe that . . .'

'Then we've got to find whoever it was!'

Poirot murmured:

'We shall not have to look far, I fancy.'

'Do you mean you *know*?'

'I have a very shrewd idea.'

Peter Lord said slowly:

'Then your minions who made inquiries in Germany *did* bring you something . . .'

Hercule Poirot said, tapping his forehead:

'My friend, it is all here, in my head. . . . Come, let us look over the house.'

III

They stood at last in the room where Mary Gerrard had died.

The house had a strange atmosphere in it: it seemed alive with memories and forebodings.

Peter Lord flung up one of the windows.

He said with a slight shiver:

'This place feels like a tomb . . .'

Poirot said:

'If walls could speak. . . . It is all here, is it not, here in the house—the beginning of the whole story.'

He paused and then said softly:

'It was here in this room that Mary Gerrard died.'

Peter Lord said:

'They found her sitting in that chair by the window. . . .'

Hercule Poirot said thoughtfully:

'A young girl—beautiful—romantic? Did she scheme and intrigue? Was she a superior person who gave herself airs? Was she gentle and sweet, with no thought of intrigue . . . just a young thing beginning life . . . a girl like a flower? . . .'

'Whatever she was,' said Peter Lord, 'someone wished her dead.'

Hercule Poirot murmured:

'I wonder . . .'

Lord stared at him.

'What do you mean?'

Poirot shook his head.

'Not yet.'

He turned about.

'We have been all through the house. We have seen all that there is to be seen here. Let us go down to the Lodge.'

Here again all was in order: the rooms dusty, but neat and

145

emptied of personal possessions. The two men stayed only a few minutes. As they came out into the sun, Poirot touched the leaves of a pillar rose growing up a trellis. It was pink and sweet-scented.

He murmured:

'Do you know the name of this rose? It is Zephyrine Drouhin, my friend.'

Peter Lord said irritably:

'What of it?'

Hercule Poirot said:

'When I saw Elinor Carlisle, she spoke to me of roses. It was then that I began to see—not daylight, but the little glimpse of light that one gets in a train when one is about to come out of a tunnel. It is not so much daylight, but the promise of daylight.'

Peter Lord said harshly:

'What did she tell you?'

'She told me of her childhood, of playing here in this garden, and of how she and Roderick Welman were on different sides. They were enemies, for he preferred the white rose of York—cold and austere—and she, so she told me, loved red roses, the red rose of Lancaster. Red roses that have scent and colour and passion and warmth. And that, my friend, is the difference between Elinor Carlisle and Roderick Welman.'

Peter Lord said:

'Does that explain—anything?'

Poirot said:

'It explains Elinor Carlisle—who is passionate and proud and who loved desperately a man who was incapable of loving her . . .'

Peter Lord said:

'I don't understand you . . .'

Poirot said:

'But I understand *her* . . . I understand both of them. Now, my friend, we will go back once more to that little clearing in the shrubbery.'

They went there in silence. Peter Lord's freckled face was troubled and angry.

When they came to the spot, Poirot stood motionless for some time, and Peter Lord watched him.

Then suddenly the little detective gave a vexed sigh.

He said:

'It is so simple, really. Do you not see, my friend, the fatal fallacy in your reasoning? According to your theory someone, a man, presumably, who had known Mary Gerrard in Germany came here intent on killing her. But *look*, my friend, *look*! Use the two eyes of your body, since the eyes of the mind do not seem to serve you. What do you see from here: a window, is it not? And at that window—a girl. A girl cutting sandwiches. That is to say, Elinor Carlisle. But think for a minute of this: *What on earth was to tell the watching man that those sandwiches were going to be offered to Mary Gerrard?* No one knew that *but Elinor Carlisle—herself—nobody!* Not even Mary Gerrard, nor Nurse Hopkins.

'So what follows—if a man stood here watching, and if he afterwards went to that window and climbed in and tampered with the sandwiches? What did he think and believe? He thought, he must have thought, *that the sandwiches were to be eaten by Elinor Carlisle herself....*'

CHAPTER THIRTEEN

Poirot knocked at the door of Nurse Hopkins' cottage. She opened it to him with her mouth full of Bath bun.

She said sharply:

'Well, Mr. Poirot, what do you want *now*?'

'I may enter?'

Somewhat grudgingly Nurse Hopkins drew back and Poirot was permitted to cross the threshold. Nurse Hopkins was hospitable with the teapot, and a minute later Poirot was regarding with some dismay a cup of inky beverage.

'Just made—nice and strong!' said Nurse Hopkins.

Poirot stirred his tea cautiously and took one heroic sip.

He said:

'Have you any idea why I have come here?'

'I couldn't say, I'm sure, until you tell me. I don't profess to be a mind-reader.'

'I have come to ask you for the truth.'

Nurse Hopkins uprose in wrath.

'And what's the meaning of that, I should like to know? A truthful woman I've always been. Not one to shield myself in any way. I spoke up about that missing tube of morphine at

147

the inquest when many a one in my place would have sat tight and said nothing. For well enough did I know that I should get censured for carelessness in leaving my case about; and, after all, it's a thing might happen to anybody! I was blamed for that—and it won't do me any good in my profession, I can tell you. But that didn't make any difference to me! I knew something that had a bearing on the case, and so I spoke out. And I'll thank you, Mr. Poirot, to keep any nasty insinuations to yourself! There's not a thing about Mary Gerrard's death that I haven't been open and above-board as daylight about, and if *you* think differently, I'd be obliged if you'd give chapter and verse for it! I've concealed nothing—nothing at all! And I'm prepared to take the oath and stand up in court and say so.'

Poirot did not attempt to interrupt. He knew only too well the technique of dealing with an angry woman. He allowed Nurse Hopkins to flare up and simmer down. Then he spoke —quietly and mildly.

He said:

'I did not suggest that there is anything about the crime which you have not told.'

'Then what did you suggest, I'd like to know?'

'I asked you to tell the truth—not about the death, but about the *life* of Mary Gerrard.'

'Oh!' Nurse Hopkins seemed momentarily taken aback. She said, 'So that's what you're getting at? But it's got nothing to do with the murder.'

'I did not say that it had. I said that you were withholding knowledge concerning her.'

'Why shouldn't I—if it's nothing to do with the crime?'

Poirot shrugged his shoulders.

'Why should you?'

Nurse Hopkins, very red in the face, said:

'Because it's common decency! They're all dead now—everyone concerned. And it's no business of anyone else's!'

'If it is only surmise—perhaps not. But if you have *actual knowledge*, that is different.'

Nurse Hopkins said slowly:

'I don't know exactly what you mean . . .'

Poirot said:

'I will help you. I have had hints from Nurse O'Brien and I have had a long conversation with Mrs. Slattery, who has a very good memory for events that happened over twenty years ago. I will tell you exactly what I have learned. Well, over twenty years ago there was a love-affair between two people. One of them was Mrs. Welman, who had been a widow for some years and who was a woman capable of a deep and passionate love. The other party was Sir Lewis Rycroft, who had the great misfortune to have a wife who was hopelessly insane. The law in those days gave no promise of relief by divorce, and Lady Rycroft, whose physical health was excellent, might live to be ninety. The *liaison* between those two people was, I think, guessed at, but they were both discreet and careful to keep up appearances. Then Sir Lewis Rycroft was killed in action.'

'Well?' said Nurse Hopkins.

'I suggest,' said Poirot, 'that there was a child born after his death, and that that child was Mary Gerrard.'

Nurse Hopkins said:

'You seem to know all about it!'

Poirot said:

'That is what I *think*. But it is possible that you have got definite proof that that is so.'

Nurse Hopkins sat silent a minute or two, frowning, then abruptly she rose, went across the room, opened a drawer and took out an envelope. She brought it across to Poirot.

She said:

'I'll tell you how this came into my hands. Mind, I'd had my suspicions. The way Mrs. Welman looked at the girl, for one thing, and then hearing the gossip on top of it. And old Gerrard told me when he was ill that Mary wasn't his daughter.

'Well, after Mary died I finished clearing up the Lodge, and in a drawer amongst some of the old man's things I came across this letter. You see what's written on it.'

Poirot read the superscription written in faded ink:

'*For Mary—to be sent to her after my death.*'

Poirot said:

'This writing is not recent?'

'It wasn't Gerrard who wrote that,' explained Nurse Hopkins. 'It was Mary's mother, who died fourteen years ago. She meant this for the girl, but the old man kept it among his things and so she never saw it—and I'm thankful she didn't! She was able to hold up her head to the end, and she'd no cause to feel ashamed.'

She paused and then said:

'Well, it was sealed up, but when I found it I'll admit to you that I opened it and read it then and there, which I dare say I should not have done. But Mary was dead, and I guessed more or less at what was inside it and I didn't see that it was any concern of anyone else's. All the same, I haven't liked to destroy it, because I didn't feel somehow it would be right to do that. But, there, you'd better read it yourself.'

Poirot drew out the sheet of paper covered in small angular writing:

'This is the truth I've written down here in case it should ever be needed. I was lady's maid to Mrs. Welman at Hunterbury, and very kind to me she was. I got into trouble, and she stood by me and took me back into her service when it was all over; but the baby died. My mistress and Sir Lewis Rycroft were fond of each other, but they couldn't marry, because he had a wife already and she was in a madhouse, poor lady. He was a fine gentleman and devoted to Mrs. Welman. He was killed, and she told me soon after that she was going to have a child. After that she went up to Scotland and took me with her. The child was born there—at Ardlochrie. Bob Gerrard, who had washed his hands of me and flung me off when I had my trouble, had been writing to me again. The arrangement was that we should marry and live at the Lodge and he should think that the baby was mine. If we lived on the place it would seem natural that Mrs. Welman should be interested in the child and she'd see to educating her and giving her a place in the world. She thought it would be better for Mary never to know the truth. Mrs. Welman gave us both a handsome sum of money; but I would have helped her without that. I've been quite happy with Bob, but he never took to Mary. I've held my tongue and never said anything to anybody, but I think it's right in case I die that I should put this down in black and white.

'ELIZA GERRARD (born ELIZA RILEY).'

Hercule Poirot drew a deep breath and folded up the letter again.

Nurse Hopkins said anxiously:

'What are you going to do about it? They're all dead now! It's no good raking up these things. Everyone looked up to

Mrs. Welman in these parts; there's never been anything said against her. All this old scandal—it would be cruel. The same with Mary. She was a sweet girl. Why should anyone have to know she was a bastard? Let the dead rest in peace in their graves, that's what I say.'

Poirot said:

'One has to consider the living.'

Nurse Hopkins said:

'But this has got nothing to do with the murder.'

Hercule Poirot said gravely:

'It may have a great deal to do with it.'

He went out of the cottage, leaving Nurse Hopkins with her mouth open, staring after him.

He had walked some way when he became aware of hesitating footsteps just behind him. He stopped and turned round.

It was Horlick, the young gardener from Hunterbury. He was looking the picture of embarrassment and twisting his cap round and round in his hands.

'Excuse me, sir. Could I have a word with you?'

Horlick spoke with a kind of gulp.

'Certainly. What is it?'

Horlick twisted the cap even more fiercely. He said, averting his eyes and looking the picture of misery and embarrassment:

'It's about that car.'

'The car that was outside the back gate that morning?'

'Yes, sir. Dr. Lord said this morning that it wasn't his car—*but it was, sir.*'

'You know that for a fact?'

'Yes, sir. Because of the number, sir. It was MSS 2022. I noticed it particular—MSS 2022. You see, we know it in the village, and always call it Miss Tou-Tou! I'm quite sure of it, sir.'

Poirot said with a faint smile:

'But Dr. Lord says he was over at Withenbury that morning.'

Horlick said miserably:

'Yes, sir. I heard him. But it *was* his car, sir. . . . I'll take my oath on that.'

Poirot said gently:

'Thank you, Horlick, that's just exactly what you may have to do. . . .'

PART THREE

CHAPTER ONE

I

Was it very hot in the court? Or very cold? Elinor Carlisle could not be quite sure. Sometimes she felt burning, as though with fever, and immediately after she shivered.

She had not heard the end of the Prosecuting Counsel's speech. She had gone back to the past—gone slowly through the whole business again, from the day when that miserable letter came to the moment when that smooth-faced police officer had said with horrible fluency:

'You are Elinor Katharine Carlisle. I have here a warrant for your arrest upon the charge of murdering Mary Gerrard by administering poison to her on the 27th of July last, and I must warn you that anything you say will be taken down in writing and may be used as evidence at your trial.'

Horrible, frightening fluency. . . . She felt caught up in a smooth-running, well-oiled machine—inhuman, passionless.

And now here she was, standing in the dock in the open glare of publicity, with hundreds of eyes that were neither impersonal nor inhuman, feasting upon her and gloating . . .

Only the jury did not look at her. Embarrassed, they kept their eyes studiously turned away. . . . She thought: 'It's because—soon—they know what they're going to say . . .'

II

Dr. Lord was giving evidence. Was this Peter Lord—that freckled, cheery young doctor who had been so kind and so friendly at Hunterbury? He was very stiff now. Sternly professional. His answers came monotonously: He had been summoned by telephone to Hunterbury Hall; too late for anything to be done; Mary Gerrard had died a few minutes after his arrival; death consistent, in his opinion, with morphia poisoning in one of its less common forms—the 'foudroyante' variety.

153

Sir Edwin Bulmer rose to cross-examine.

'You were the late Mrs. Welman's regular medical attendant?'

'I was.'

'During your visits to Hunterbury in June last, you had occasion to see the accused and Mary Gerrard together?'

'Several times.'

'What would you say was the manner of the accused to Mary Gerrard?'

'Perfectly pleasant and natural.'

Sir Edwin Bulmer said with a slight disdainful smile:

'You never saw any signs of this "jealous hatred" we have heard so much about?'

Peter Lord, his jaw set, said firmly:

'No.'

Elinor thought:

'But he did—he did. . . . He told a lie for me there. . . . He knew. . . .'

Peter Lord was succeeded by the police surgeon. His evidence was longer, more detailed. Death was due to morphia poisoning of the 'foudroyante' variety. Would he kindly explain that term? With some enjoyment he did so. Death from morphine poisoning might occur in several different ways. The most common was a period of intense excitement followed by drowsiness and narcosis, pupils of eyes contracted. Another not so common form had been named by the French, 'foudroyante.' In these cases deep sleep supervened in a very short time—about ten minutes; the pupils of the eyes were usually dilated. . . .

III

The court had adjourned and sat again. There had been some hours of expert medical testimony.

Dr. Alan Garcia, the distinguished analyst, full of learned terms, spoke with gusto of the stomach contents: Bread, fish paste, tea, presence of morphia . . . more learned terms and various decimal points. Amount taken by the deceased estimated to be about four grains. Fatal dose could be as low as one grain.

Sir Edwin rose, still bland.

'I should like to get it quite clear. You found in the

154

stomach nothing but bread, butter, fish paste, tea and morphia. There were no other foodstuffs?'

'None.'

'That is to say, the deceased had eaten nothing but sandwiches and tea for some considerable time?'

'That is so.'

'Was there anything to show in what particular vehicle the morphia had been administered?'

'I don't quite understand.'

'I will simplify that question. The morphia could have been taken in the fish paste, or in the bread, or in the butter on the bread, or in the tea, or in the milk that had been added to the tea?'

'Certainly.'

'There was no special evidence that the morphia was in the fish paste rather than in any of the other mediums?'

'No.'

'And, in fact, the morphia *might* have been taken separately —that is to say, not in any vehicle at all? It could have been simply swallowed in its tablet form?'

'That is so, of course.'

Sir Edwin sat down.

Sir Samuel re-examined.

'Nevertheless, you are of the opinion that, however the morphia was taken, it was taken at the same time as the other food and drink?'

'Yes.'

'Thank you.'

I V

Inspector Brill had taken the oath with mechanical fluency. He stood there, soldierly and stolid, reeling off his evidence with practised ease.

'Summoned to the house. . . . The accused said, "It must have been bad fish paste." . . . search of the premises . . . one jar of fish paste washed out was standing on the draining-board in the pantry, another half full . . . further search of pantry kitchen. . . .'

'What did you find?'

'In a crack behind the table, between the floorboards, I found a tiny scrap of paper.'

The exhibit went to the jury.

IC TABLETS.
orphin. Hydr
gr. 1/2

'What did you take it to be?'

'A fragment torn off a printed label—such as are used on glass tubes of morphia.'

Counsel for the Defence arose with leisurely ease.

He said:

'You found this scrap in a crack in the flooring?'

'Yes.'

'Part of a label?'

'Yes.'

'Did you find the rest of that label?'

'No.'

'You did not find any glass tube or any bottle to which that label might have been affixed?'

'No.'

'What was the state of that scrap of paper when you found it? Was it clean or dirty?'

'It was quite fresh.'

'What do you mean, quite fresh?'

'There was surface dust on it from the flooring, but it was quite clean otherwise.'

'It could not have been there for any length of time?'

'No, it had found its way there quite recently.'

'You would say, then, that it had come there on the actual day you found it—not earlier?'

'Yes.'

With a grunt Sir Edwin sat down.

v

Nurse Hopkins in the box, her face red and self-righteous.

All the same, Elinor thought, Nurse Hopkins was not so frightening as Inspector Brill. It was the inhumanity of Inspector Brill that was so paralysing. He was so definitely part of a great machine. Nurse Hopkins had human passions, prejudices.

'Your name is Jessie Hopkins?'

'Yes.'

'You are a certificated District Nurse and you reside at Rose Cottage, Hunterbury?'

'Yes.'

'Where were you on the 28th of June last?'

'I was at Hunterbury Hall.'

'You had been sent for?'

'Yes. Mrs. Welman had had a stroke—the second. I went to assist Nurse O'Brien until a second nurse could be found.'

'Did you take a small attaché-case with you?'

'Yes.'

'Tell the jury what was in it.'

'Bandages, dressings, a hypodermic syringe and certain drugs, including a tube of morphine hydrochloride.'

'For what purpose was it there?'

'One of the cases in the village had to have hypodermic injections of morphia morning and evening.'

'What were the contents of the tube?'

'There were twenty tablets, each containing half-grain Morphine Hydrochloride.'

'What did you do with your attaché-case?'

'I laid it down in the hall.'

'That was on the evening of the 28th. When did you next have occasion to look in the case?'

'The following morning about nine o'clock, just as I was preparing to leave the house.'

'Was anything missing?'

'The tube of morphine was missing.'

'Did you mention this loss?'

'I spoke of it to Nurse O'Brien, the nurse in charge of the patient.'

'This case was lying in the hall, where people were in the habit of passing to and fro?'

'Yes.'

Sir Samuel paused. Then he said:

'You knew the dead girl Mary Gerrard intimately?'

'Yes.'

'What was your opinion of her?'

'She was a very sweet girl—and a good girl.'

'Was she of a happy disposition?'

'Very happy.'

'She had no troubles that you know of?'

'No.'

'At the time of her death was there anything whatever to worry her or make her unhappy about the future?'

'Nothing.'

'She would have had no reason to have taken her own life?'

'No reason at all.'

It went on and on—the damning story. How Nurse Hopkins had accompanied Mary to the Lodge, the appearance of Elinor, her excitable manner, the invitation to sandwiches, the plate being handed first to Mary. Elinor's suggestion that everything be washed up, and her further suggestion that Nurse Hopkins should come upstairs with her and assist in sorting out clothes.

There were frequent interruptions and objections from Sir Edwin Bulmer.

Elinor thought:

'Yes, it's all true—and she believes it. She's certain I did it. And every word she says is the truth—that's what's so horrible. It's all true.'

Once more, as she looked across the court, she saw the face of Hercule Poirot regarding her thoughtfully—almost kindly. *Seeing her with too much knowledge.* . . .

The piece of cardboard with the scrap of label pasted on to it was handed to the witness.

'Do you know what this is?'

'It's a bit of a label.'

'Can you tell the jury what label?'

'Yes—it's a part of a label off a tube of hypodermic tablets. Morphine tablets $\frac{1}{2}$-grain—like the one I lost.'

'You are sure of that?'

'Of course I'm sure. It's off my tube.'

The judge said:

'Is there any special mark on it by which you can identify it as the label of the tube you lost?'

'No, my lord, but it must be the same.'

'Actually, all you can say is that it is exactly similar?'

'Well, yes, that's what I mean.'

The court adjourned.

CHAPTER TWO

I

It was another day.

Sir Edwin Bulmer was on his feet cross-examining. He was not at all bland now. He said sharply:

'This attaché-case we've heard so much about. On June 28th it was left in the main hall of Hunterbury all night?'

Nurse Hopkins agreed:

'Yes.'

'Rather a careless thing to do, wasn't it?'

Nurse Hopkins flushed.

'Yes, I suppose it was.'

'Are you in the habit of leaving dangerous drugs lying about where anyone could get at 'em?'

'No, of course not.'

'Oh! you're not? But you did it on this occasion?'

'Yes.'

'And it's a fact, isn't it, that *anybody in the house* could have got at that morphia if they'd wanted to?'

'I suppose so.'

'No suppose about it. It is so, isn't it?'

'Well—yes.'

'It wasn't only Miss Carlisle who could have got at it? Any of the servants could. Or Dr. Lord. Or Mr. Roderick Welman. Or Nurse O'Brien. Or Mary Gerrard herself.'

'I suppose so—yes.'

'It is so, isn't it?'

'Yes.'

'Was anyone aware you'd got morphia in that case?'

'I don't know.'

'Well, did you talk about it to anyone?'

'No.'

'So, as a matter of fact, Miss Carlisle couldn't have known that there was any morphia there?'

'She might have looked to see.'

'That's very unlikely, isn't it?'

'I don't know, I'm sure.'

'There were people who'd be more likely to know about the

morphia than Miss Carlisle. Dr. Lord, for instance. He'd know. You were administering this morphia under his orders, weren't you?'

'Of course.'

'Mary Gerrard knew you had it there, too?'

'No, she didn't.'

'She was often in your cottage, wasn't she?'

'Not very often.'

'I suggest to you that she was there very frequently, and that she, of all the people in the house, would be the most likely to guess that there was morphia in your case.'

'I don't agree.'

Sir Edwin paused a minute.

'You told Nurse O'Brien in the morning that the morphia was missing?'

'Yes.'

'I put it to you that what you really said was: "I have left the morphia at home. I shall have to go back for it."'

'No, I didn't.'

'You didn't suggest that the morphia had been left on the mantelpiece in your cottage?'

'Well, when I couldn't find it I thought that must have been what had happened.'

'In fact, you didn't really know what you'd done with it!'

'Yes, I did. I put it in the case.'

'Then why did you suggest on the morning of June 29th that you had left it at home?'

'Because I thought I might have done.'

'I put it to you that you're a very careless woman.'

'That's not true.'

'You make rather inaccurate statements sometimes, don't you?'

'No, I don't. I'm very careful what I say.'

'Did you make a remark about a prick from a rose tree on July 27th—the day of Mary Gerrard's death?'

'I don't see what that's got to do with it!'

The judge said:

'Is that relevant, Sir Edwin?'

'Yes, my lord, it is an essential part of the defence, and I intend to call witnesses to prove that that statement was a lie.'

He resumed:

'Do you still say you pricked your wrist on a rose tree on July 27th?'

160

'Yes, I did.'

Nurse Hopkins looked defiant.

'When did you do that?'

'Just before leaving the Lodge and coming up to the house on the morning of July 27th.'

Sir Edwin said sceptically:

'And what rose tree was this?'

'A climbing one just outside the Lodge, with pink flowers.'

'You're sure of that?'

'I'm quite sure.'

Sir Edwin paused and then asked:

'You persist in saying the morphia was in the attaché-case when you came to Hunterbury on June 28th?'

'I do. I had it with me.'

'Supposing that presently Nurse O'Brien goes into the box and swears that you said you had probably left it at home?'

'It was in my case. I'm sure of it.'

Sir Edwin sighed.

'You didn't feel at all uneasy about the disappearance of the morphia?'

'Not—uneasy—no.'

'Oh, so you were quite at ease, notwithstanding the fact that a large quantity of a dangerous drug had disappeared?'

'I didn't think at the time anyone had taken it.'

'I see. You just couldn't remember for the moment what you had done with it?'

'Not at all. It was in the case.'

'Twenty half-grain tablets—that is, ten grains of morphia. Enough to kill several people, isn't it?'

'Yes.'

'But you are not uneasy—and you don't even report the loss officially?'

'I thought it was all right.'

'I put it to you that if the morphia had really disappeared the way it did you would have been bound, as a conscientious person, to report the loss officially.'

Nurse Hopkins, very red in the face, said:

'Well, I didn't.'

'That was surely a piece of criminal carelessness on your part? You don't seem to take your responsibilities very seriously. Did you often mislay these dangerous drugs?'

'It never happened before.'

It went on for some minutes. Nurse Hopkins, flustered, red

in the face, contradicting herself . . . an easy prey to Sir Edwin's skill.

'Is it a fact that on Thursday, July 6th, the dead girl, Mary Gerrard, made a will?'

'She did.'

'Why did she do that?'

'Because she thought it was the proper thing to do. And so it was.'

'Are you sure it wasn't because she was depressed and uncertain about her future?'

'Nonsense.'

'It showed, though, that the idea of death was present in her mind—that she was brooding on the subject.'

'Not at all. She just thought it was the proper thing to do.'

'Is this the will? Signed by Mary Gerrard, witnessed by Emily Biggs and Roger Wade, confectioners' assistants, and leaving everything of which she died possessed to Mary Riley, sister of Eliza Riley?'

'That's right.'

It was handed to the jury.

'To your knowledge, had Mary Gerrard any property to leave?'

'Not then, she hadn't.'

'But she was shortly going to have?'

'Yes.'

'Is it not a fact that a considerable sum of money—two thousand pounds—was being given to Mary by Miss Carlisle?'

'Yes.'

'There was no compulsion on Miss Carlisle to do this? It was entirely a generous impulse on her part?'

'She did it of her own free will, yes.'

'But surely, if she had hated Mary Gerrard, as is suggested, she would not of her own free will have handed over to her a large sum of money.'

'That's as may be.'

'What do you mean by that answer?'

'I don't mean anything.'

'Exactly. Now, had you heard any local gossip about Mary Gerrard and Mr. Roderick Welman?'

'He was sweet on her.'

'Have you any evidence of that?'

'I just knew it, that's all.'

'Oh—you "just knew it." That's not very convincing to the jury, I'm afraid. Did you say on one occasion Mary would have nothing to do with him because he was engaged to Miss Elinor and she said the same to him in London?'

'That's what she told me.'

Sir Samuel Attenbury re-examined:

'When Mary Gerrard was discussing with you the wording of this will, did the accused look in through the window?'

'Yes, she did.'

'What did she say?'

'She said, "So you're making your will, Mary. That's funny." And she laughed. Laughed and laughed. And it's my opinion,' said the witness viciously, 'that it was at that moment the idea came into her head. The idea of making away with the girl! She'd murder in her heart that very minute.'

The judge spoke sharply:

'Confine yourself to answering the questions that are asked you. The last part of that answer is to be struck out. . . .'

Elinor thought:

'How queer. . . . When anyone says what's true, they strike it out. . . .'

She wanted to laugh hysterically.

II

Nurse O'Brien was in the box.

'On the morning of June 29th did Nurse Hopkins make a statement to you?'

'Yes. She said she had a tube of morphine hydrochloride missing from her case.'

'What did you do?'

'I helped her to hunt for it.'

'But you could not find it?'

'No.'

'To your knowledge, was the case left overnight in the hall?'

'It was.'

'Mr. Welman and the accused were both staying in the house at the time of Mrs. Welman's death—that is, on June 28th to 29th?'

'Yes.'

'Will you tell us of an incident that occurred on June 29th —the day after Mrs. Welman's death?'

'I saw Mr. Roderick Welman with Mary Gerrard. He was telling her he loved her, and he tried to kiss her.'

'He was at the time engaged to the accused?'

'Yes.'

'What happened next?'

'Mary told him to think shame of himself, and him engaged to Miss Elinor!'

'In your opinion, what was the feeling of the accused towards Mary Gerrard?'

'She hated her. She would look after her as though she'd like to destroy her.'

Sir Edwin jumped up.

Elinor thought: 'Why do they wrangle about it? What does it *matter*?'

Sir Edwin Bulmer cross-examined:

'Is it not a fact that Nurse Hopkins said she thought she had left the morphia at home?'

'Well, you see, it was this way: After——'

'Kindly answer my question. Did she not say that she had probably left the morphia at home?'

'Yes.'

'She was not really worried at the time about it?'

'No, not then.'

'Because she thought she had left it at home. So naturally she was not uneasy.'

'She couldn't imagine anyone taking it?'

'Exactly. It wasn't till after Mary Gerrard's death from morphia that her imagination got to work.'

The judge interrupted:

'I think, Sir Edwin, that you have already been over that point with the former witness.'

'As your lordship pleases.'

'Now, regarding the attitude of the accused to Mary Gerrard, there was no quarrel between them at any time?'

'No quarrel, no.'

'Miss Carlisle was always quite pleasant to the girl?'

'Yes. 'Twas the way she looked at her.'

'Yes—yes—yes. But we can't go by that sort of thing. You're Irish, I think?'

'I am that.'

'And the Irish have rather a vivid imagination, haven't they?'

Nurse O'Brien cried excitedly:

'Every word I've told you is the truth.'

III

Mr. Abbott, the grocer, in the box. Flustered—unsure of himself (slightly thrilled, though, at his importance). His evidence was short. The purchase of two pots of fish paste. The accused had said, 'There's a lot of food poisoning with fish paste.' She had seemed excited and queer.

No cross-examination.

CHAPTER THREE

I

Opening speech for the Defence:

'Gentlemen of the Jury, I might, if I like, submit to you that there is no case against the accused. The onus of proof is on the Prosecution, and so far, in my opinion—and, I have no doubt, yours—they have proved exactly nothing at all! The Prosecution avers that Elinor Carlisle, having obtained possession of morphine (which everyone else in the house had had equal opportunity of purloining, and as to which there exists considerable doubt whether it was ever in the house at all), proceeds to poison Mary Gerrard. Here the Prosecution has relied solely on opportunity. It has sought to prove motive, but I submit that that is just what it has not been able to do. For, members of the jury, there is no motive! The Prosecution has spoken of a broken engagement. I ask you—a broken engagement! If a broken engagement is a cause for murder, why are we not having murders committed every day? And this engagement, mark you, was not an affair of desperate passion, it was an engagement entered into mainly for family reasons. Miss Carlisle and Mr. Welman had grown up together; they had always been fond of each other, and gradually they drifted into a warmer attachment; but I intend to prove to you it was at best a very luke-warm affair.'

(Oh, Roddy—Roddy. A luke-warm affair?)

'Moreover, this engagement was broken off, not by Mr. Welman—but by the prisoner. I submit to you that the engage-

165

ment between Elinor Carlisle and Roderick Welman was entered into mainly to please old Mrs. Welman. When she died, both parties realised that their feelings were not strong enough to justify them in entering upon matrimony. They remained, however, good friends. Moreover, Elinor Carlisle, who had inherited her aunt's fortune, in the kindliness of her nature, was planning to settle a considerable sum of money on Mary Gerrard. And this is the girl she is accused of poisoning! The thing is farcical.

'The only thing that there is against Elinor Carlisle is the circumstances under which the poisoning took place.

'The Prosecution has said in effect:

'No one but Elinor Carlisle could have killed Mary Gerrard. Therefore they have had to search about for a possible motive. But, as I have said to you, they have been unable to find any motive because there was none.

'Now, is it true that no one but Elinor Carlisle could have killed Mary Gerrard? No, it is not. There is the possibility that Mary Gerrard committed suicide. There is the possibility that someone tampered with the sandwiches while Elinor Carlisle was out of the house at the Lodge. There is a third possibility. It is a fundamental law of evidence that if it can be shown that there is an alternative theory which is possible and consistent with the evidence, the accused must be acquitted. I propose to show you that there was another person who had not only an equal opportunity to poison Mary Gerrard, but who had a far better motive for doing so. I propose to call evidence to show you that there was another person who had access to the morphine, and who had a very good motive for killing Mary Gerrard, and I can show that that person had an equally good opportunity of doing so. I submit to you that no jury in the world will convict this woman of murder when there is no evidence against her except that of opportunity, and when it can be shown that there is not only evidence of opportunity against another person, but an overwhelming motive. I shall also call witnesses to prove that there has been deliberate perjury on the part of one of the witnesses for the Crown. But first I will call the prisoner, that she may tell you her own story, and that you may see for yourself how entirely unfounded the charges against her are.'

She had taken the oath. She was answering Sir Edwin's questions in a low voice. The judge leaned forward. He told her to speak louder. . . .

Sir Edwin was talking gently and encouragingly—all the questions to which she had rehearsed the answers.

'You were fond of Roderick Welman?'

'Very fond. He was like a brother to me—or a cousin. I always thought of him as a cousin.'

The engagement . . . drifted into it . . . very pleasant to marry someone you had known all your life. . . .

'Not, perhaps, what might be called a passionate affair?'

(Passionate? Oh, Roddy. . . .)

'Well, no . . . you see we knew each other so well . . .'

'After the death of Mrs. Welman was there a slightly strained feeling between you?'

'Yes, there was.'

'How did you account for this?'

'I think it was partly the money.'

'The money?'

'Yes. Roderick felt uncomfortable. He thought people might think he was marrying me for that . . .'

'The engagement was not broken off on account of Mary Gerrard?'

'I did think Roderick was rather taken with her, but I didn't believe it was anything serious.'

'Would you have been upset if it had been?'

'Oh, no. I should have thought it rather unsuitable, that is all.'

'Now, Miss Carlisle. Did you or did you not take a tube of morphine from Nurse Hopkins' attaché-case on June 28th?'

'I did not.'

'Have you at any time had morphine in your possession?'

'Never.'

'Were you aware that your aunt had not made a will?'

'No. It came as a great surprise to me.'

'Did you think she was trying to convey to you a message on the night of June 28th when she died?'

'I understood that she had made no provision for Mary Gerrard, and was anxious to do so.'

'And in order to carry out her wishes, you yourself were prepared to settle a sum of money on the girl?'

'Yes. I wanted to carry out Aunt Laura's wishes. And I was grateful for the kindness Mary had shown to my aunt.'

'On July 26th did you come down from London to Maidensford and stay at the King's Arms?'

'Yes.'

'What was your purpose in coming down?'

'I had an offer for the house, and the man who had bought it wanted possession as quickly as possible. I had to look through my aunt's personal things and settle things up generally.'

'Did you buy various provisions on your way to the Hall on July 27th?'

'Yes. I thought it would be easier to have a picnic lunch there than to come back to the village.'

'Did you then go on to the house, and did you sort through your aunt's personal effects?'

'I did.'

'And after that?'

'I came down to the pantry and cut some sandwiches. I then went down to the Lodge and invited the District Nurse and Mary Gerrard to come up to the house.'

'Why did you do this?'

'I wished to save them a hot walk back to the village and back again to the Lodge.'

'It was, in fact, a natural and kindly action on your part. Did they accept the invitation?'

'Yes. They walked up to the house with me.'

'Where were the sandwiches you had cut?'

'I left them in the pantry on a plate.'

'Was the window open?'

'Yes.'

'Anyone could have got into the pantry while you were absent?'

'Certainly.'

'If anybody had observed you from outside while you were cutting the sandwiches, what would they have thought?'

'I suppose that I was preparing to have a picnic lunch.'

'They could not know, could they, that anyone was to share the lunch?'

'No. The idea of inviting the other two only came to me when I saw what a quantity of food I had.'

168

'So that if anyone had entered the house during your absence and placed morphine in one of those sandwiches, it would be *you* they were attempting to poison?'

'Well, yes, it would.'

'What happened when you had all arrived back at the house?'

'We went into the morning-room. I fetched the sandwiches and handed them to the other two.'

'Did you drink anything with them?'

'I drank water. There was beer on a table; but Nurse Hopkins and Mary preferred tea. Nurse Hopkins went into the pantry and made it. She brought it in on a tray and Mary poured it out.'

'Did you have any?'

'No.'

'But Mary Gerrard and Nurse Hopkins both drank tea?'

'Yes.'

'What happened next?'

'Nurse Hopkins went and turned the gas-ring off.'

'Leaving you alone with Mary Gerrard?'

'Yes.'

'What happened next?'

'After a few minutes I picked up the tray and the sandwich plate and carried them into the pantry. Nurse Hopkins was there, and we washed them together.'

'Did Nurse Hopkins have her cuffs off at the time?'

'Yes. She was washing the things, while I dried them.'

'Did you make a certain remark to her about a scratch on her wrist?'

'I asked her if she had pricked herself.'

'What did she reply?'

'She said, "It was a thorn from the rose tree outside the Lodge. I'll get it out presently."'

'What was her manner at the time?'

'I think she was feeling the heat. She was perspiring and her face was a queer colour.'

'What happened after that?'

'We went upstairs, and she helped me with my aunt's things.'

'What time was it when you went downstairs again?'

'It must have been an hour later.'

'Where was Mary Gerrard?'

'She was sitting in the morning-room. She was breathing very queerly and was in a coma. I rang up the doctor on

Nurse Hopkins' instructions. He arrived just before she died.'

Sir Edwin squared his shoulders dramatically.

'Miss Carlisle, did you kill Mary Gerrard?'

(That's your cue! Head up, eyes straight.)

'No!'

III

Sir Samuel Attenbury. A sick beating at one's heart. Now—now she was at the mercy of an enemy! No more gentleness, no more questions to which she knew the answers!

But he began quite mildly.

'You were engaged to be married, you have told us, to Mr. Roderick Welman?'

'Yes.'

'You were fond of him?'

'Very fond.'

'I put it to you that you were deeply in love with Roderick Welman and that you were wildly jealous of his love for Mary Gerrard?'

'No.' (Did it sound properly indignant, that "no"?)

Sir Samuel said menacingly:

'I put it to you that you deliberately planned to put this girl out of the way, in the hope that Roderick Welman would return to you.'

'Certainly not.' (Disdainful—a little weary. That was better.)

The questions went on. It was just like a dream . . . a bad dream . . . a nightmare . . .

Question after question . . . horrible, hurting questions. . . . Some of them she was prepared for, some took her unawares. . . .

Always trying to remember her part. Never once to let go, to say:

'Yes, I did hate her. . . . Yes, I did want her dead. . . . Yes, all the time I was cutting the sandwiches I was thinking of her dying. . . .'

To remain calm and cool and answer as briefly and passionlessly as possible . . .

Fighting . . .

Fighting every inch of the way . . .

Over now. . . . The horrible man with the Jewish nose was

170

sitting down. And the kindly, unctuous voice of Sir Edwin Bulmer was asking a few more questions. Easy, pleasant questions, designed to remove any bad impression she might have made under cross-examination. . . .

She was back again in the dock. Looking at the jury, wondering. . . .

IV

Roddy. Roddy standing there, blinking a little, hating it all. Roddy—looking somehow—not quite *real*.

But nothing's real any more. Everything is whirling round in a devilish way. Black's white, and top is bottom and east is west. . . . And I'm not Elinor Carlisle; I'm 'the accused.' And, whether they hang me or whether they let me go, nothing will ever be the same again. If there were just something—just one sane thing to hold on to . . .

(Peter Lord's face, perhaps, with its freckles and its extraordinary air of being just the same as usual. . . .)

Where had Sir Edwin got to now?

'Will you tell us what were the state of Miss Carlisle's feelings towards you?'

Roddy answered in his precise voice:

'I should say she was deeply attached to me, but certainly not passionately in love with me.'

'You considered your engagement satisfactory?'

'Oh, quite. We had a good deal in common.'

'Will you tell the jury, Mr. Welman, exactly why that engagement was broken off?'

'Well, after Mrs. Welman died it pulled us up, I think, with a bit of a shock. I didn't like the idea of marrying a rich woman when I myself was penniless. Actually the engagement was dissolved by mutual consent. We were both rather relieved.'

'Now, will you tell us just what your relations were with Mary Gerrard?'

(Oh, Roddy, poor Roddy, how you must hate all this!)

'I thought her very lovely.'

'Were you in love with her?'

'Just a little.'

'When was the last time you saw her?'

'Let me see. It must have been the 5th or 6th of July.'

171

Sir Edwin said, a touch of steel in his voice:

'You saw her after that, I think.'

'No, I went abroad—to Venice and Dalmatia.'

'You returned to England—when?'

'When I received a telegram—let me see—on the 1st of August, it must have been.'

'But you were actually in England on July 27th, I think.'

'No.'

'Come, now, Mr. Welman. You are on oath, remember. Is it not a fact that your passport shows that you returned to England on July 25th and left it again on the night of the 27th?'

Sir Edwin's voice held a subtly menacing note. Elinor frowned, suddenly jerked back to reality. Why was Counsel bullying his own witness?

Roderick had turned rather pale. He was silent for a minute or two, then he said with an effort:

'Well—yes, that is so.'

'Did you go and see this girl Mary Gerrard in London on the 25th at her lodgings?'

'Yes, I did.'

'Did you ask her to marry you?'

'Er—er—yes.'

'What was her answer?'

'She refused.'

'You are not a rich man, Mr. Welman?'

'No.'

'And you are rather heavily in debt?'

'What business is that of yours?'

'Were you not aware of the fact that Miss Carlisle had left all her money to you in the event of her death?'

'This is the first I have heard of it.'

'Were you in Maidensford on the morning of July 27th?'

'I was not.'

Sir Edwin sat down.

Counsel for the Prosecution said:

'You say that in your opinion the accused was not deeply in love with you.'

'That is what I said.'

'Are you a chivalrous man, Mr. Welman?'

'I don't know what you mean.'

'If a lady were deeply in love with you and you were not in love with her, would you feel it incumbent upon you to conceal the fact?'

172

'Certainly not.'

'Where did you go to school, Mr. Welman?'

'Eton.'

Sir Samuel said with a quiet smile:

'That is all.'

V

Alfred James Wargrave.

'You are a rose-grower and live at Emsworth, Berks.?'

'Yes.'

'Did you on October 20th go to Maidensford and examine a rose tree growing at the Lodge at Hunterbury Hall?'

'I did.'

'Will you describe this tree?'

'It was a climbing rose—Zephyrine Drouhin. It bears a sweetly scented pink flower. It has no thorns.'

'It would be impossible to prick oneself on a rose tree of this description?'

'It would be quite impossible. It is a thornless tree.'

No cross-examination.

VI

'You are James Arthur Littledale. You are a qualified chemist and employed by the wholesale chemists, Jenkins & Hale?'

'I am.'

'Will you tell me what this scrap of paper is?'

The exhibit was handed to him.

'It is a fragment of one of our labels.'

'What kind of label?'

'The label we attach to tubes of hypodermic tablets.'

'Is there enough here for you to say definitely what drug was in the tube to which this label was attached?'

'Yes. I should say quite definitely that the tube in question contained hypodermic tablets of Apomorphine Hydrochloride 1/20 grain.'

'Not Morphine Hydrochloride?'

'No, it could not be that.'

'Why not?'

'On such a tube the word Morphine is spelt with a capital

173

M. The end of the line of the m here, seen under my magnifying-glass, shows plainly that it is part of a small m, not a capital M.'

'Please let the jury examine it with the glass. Have you labels here to show what you mean?'

The labels were handed to the jury.

Sir Edwin resumed:

'You say this is from a tube of Apomorphine Hydrochloride? What exactly is Apomorphine Hydrochloride?'

'The formula is $C_7.H_{17}N\ O_2$. It is a derivative of morphine prepared by saponifying morphine by heating it with dilute hydrochloric acid in sealed tubes. The morphine loses one molecule of water.'

'What are the special properties of Apomorphine?'

Mr. Littledale said quietly:

'Apomorphine is the quickest and most powerful emetic known. It acts within a few minutes.'

'So if anybody had swallowed a lethal dose of morphine and were *to inject a dose of apomorphine hypodermically within a few minutes*, what would result?'

'Vomiting would take place almost immediately and the morphine would be expelled from the system.'

'Therefore, if two people were to share the same sandwich *or drink from the same pot of tea*, and one of them were then to inject a dose of apomorphine hypodermically, what would be the result, supposing the shared food or drink to have contained morphine?'

'The food or drink together with the morphine would be vomited by the person who injected the apomorphine.'

'And that person would suffer no ill-results?'

'No.'

There was suddenly a stir of excitement in court and order for silence from the judge.

VII

'You are Amelia Mary Sedley and you reside ordinarily at 17 Charles Street, Boonamba, Auckland?'

'Yes.'

'Do you know a Mrs. Draper?'

'Yes. I have known her for over twenty years.'

'Do you know her maiden name?'

'Yes. I was at her marriage. Her name was Mary Riley.'

'Is she a native of New Zealand?'

'No, she came out from England.'

'You have been in court since the beginning of these proceedings?'

'Yes, I have.'

'Have you seen this Mary Riley—or Draper—in court?'

'Yes.'

'Where did you see her?'

'Giving evidence in this box.'

'Under what name?'

'Jessie Hopkins.'

'And you are quite sure that this Jessie Hopkins is the woman you know as Mary Riley or Draper?'

'Not a doubt of it.'

A slight commotion at the back of the court.

'When did you last see Mary Draper—until to-day?'

'Five years ago. She went to England.'

Sir Edwin said with a bow:

'Your witness.'

Sir Samuel, rising with a slightly perplexed face, began:

'I suggest to you, Mrs.—Sedley, that you may be mistaken.'

'I'm not mistaken.'

'You may have been misled by a chance resemblance.'

'I know Mary Draper well enough.'

'Nurse Hopkins is a certificated District Nurse.'

'Mary Draper was a hospital nurse before her marriage.'

'You understand, do you not, that you are accusing a Crown witness of perjury?'

'I understand what I'm saying.'

VIII

'Edward John Marshall, you lived for some years in Auckland, New Zealand, and now reside at 14 Wren Street, Deptford?'

'That's right.'

'Do you know Mary Draper?'

'I've known her for years in New Zealand.'

'Have you seen her to-day in court?'

'I have. She called herself Hopkins; but it was Mrs. Draper all right.'

The judge lifted his head. He spoke in a small, clear, penetrating voice:

'It is desirable, I think, that the witness Jessie Hopkins should be recalled.'

A pause, a murmur.

'Your lordship, Jessie Hopkins left the court a few minutes ago.'

IX

'Hercule Poirot.'

Hercule Poirot entered the box, took the oath, twirled his moustache and waited, with his head a little on one side. He gave his name and address and calling.

'M. Poirot, do you recognise this document?'

'Certainly.'

'How did it originally come into your possession?'

'It was given me by the District Nurse, Nurse Hopkins.'

Sir Edwin said:

'With your permission, my lord, I will read this aloud, and it can then go to the jury.'

CHAPTER FOUR

I

Closing speech for the Defence.

'Gentlemen of the jury, the responsibility now rests with you. It is for you to say if Elinor Carlisle is to go forth free from the court. If, after the evidence you have heard, you are satisfied that Elinor Carlisle poisoned Mary Gerrard, then it is your duty to pronounce her guilty.

'But if it should seem to you that there is equally strong evidence, and perhaps far stronger evidence against another person, then it is your duty to free the accused without more ado.

'You will have realised by now that the facts of the case are very different from what they originally appeared to be.

'Yesterday, after the dramatic evidence given by M. Hercule Poirot, I called other witnesses to prove beyond any reasonable doubt that the girl Mary Gerrard was the illegitimate daughter of Laura Welman. That being true, it follows, as his lordship will doubtless instruct you, that Mrs. Welman's next of kin was not her niece, Elinor Carlisle, but her illegitimate daughter who went by the name of Mary Gerrard. And therefore Mary Gerrard at Mrs. Welman's death inherited a vast fortune. That, gentlemen, is the crux of the situation. A sum in the neighbourhood of two hundred thousand pounds was inherited by Mary Gerrard. But she herself was unaware of the fact. She was also unaware of the true identity of the woman Hopkins. You may think, gentlemen, that Mary Riley or Draper may have had some perfectly legitimate reason for changing her name to Hopkins. If so, why has she not come forward to state what the reason was?

'All that we do know is this: That at Nurse Hopkins' instigation, Mary Gerrard made a will leaving everything she had to "Mary Riley, sister of Eliza Riley." We know that Nurse Hopkins, by reason of her profession, had access to morphine and to apomorphine and was well acquainted with their properties. Furthermore, it has been proved that Nurse Hopkins was not speaking the truth when she said that her wrist had been pricked by a thorn from a thornless rose tree. Why did she lie, if it were not that she wanted hurriedly *to account for the mark just made by the hypodermic needle?* Remember, too, that the accused has stated on oath that Nurse Hopkins, when she joined her in the pantry, was looking ill, and her face was of a greenish colour—comprehensible enough if she had just been violently sick.

'I will underline yet another point: *If* Mrs. Welman had lived twenty-four hours longer, she would have made a will; and in all probability that will would have made a suitable provision for Mary Gerrard, but would not have left her the bulk of her fortune, since it was Mrs. Welman's belief that her unacknowledged daughter would be happier if she remained in another sphere of life.

'It is not for me to pronounce on the evidence against another person, except to show that this other person had equal opportunities and a far stronger motive for the murder.

'Looked at from that point of view, gentlemen of the jury, I submit to you that the case against Elinor Carlisle falls to the ground. . . .'

From Mr. Justice Beddingfield's summing-up:

'. . . You must be perfectly satisfied that this woman did, in fact, administer a dangerous dose of morphia to Mary Gerrard on July 27th. If you are not satisfied, you must acquit the prisoner.

'The Prosecution has stated that the only person who had the opportunity to administer poison to Mary Gerrard was the accused. The Defence has sought to prove that there were other alternatives. There is the theory that Mary Gerrard committed suicide, but the only evidence in support of that theory is the fact that Mary Gerrard made a will shortly before she died. There is not the slightest proof that she was depressed or unhappy or in a state of mind likely to lead her to take her own life. It has also been suggested that the morphine might have been introduced into the sandwiches by someone entering the pantry during the time that Elinor Carlisle was at the Lodge. In that case, the poison was intended for Elinor Carlisle, and Mary Gerrard's death was a mistake. The third alternative suggested by the Defence is that another person had an equal opportunity to administer morphine, and that in the latter case the poison was introduced into the tea and not into the sandwiches. In support of that theory the Defence has called the witness Littledale, who has sworn that the scrap of paper found in the pantry was part of a label on a tube containing tablets of apomorphine hydrochloride, a very powerful emetic. You have had an example of both types of labels submitted to you. In my view, the police were guilty of gross carelessness in not checking the original fragment more closely and in jumping to the conclusion that it was a morphine label.

'The witness Hopkins has stated that she pricked her wrist on a rose tree at the Lodge. The witness Wargrave has examined that tree, and it has no thorns on it. You have to decide what caused the mark on Nurse Hopkins' wrist and why she should tell a lie about it. . . .

'If the Prosecution has convinced you that the accused and no other committed the crime, then you must find the accused guilty.

'If the alternative theory suggested by the Defence is possible and consistent with the evidence, the accused must be acquitted.

'I will ask you to consider the verdict with courage and diligence, weighing only the evidence that has been put before you.'

III

Elinor was brought back into the court.

The jury filed in.

'Gentlemen of the jury, are you agreed upon your verdict?'

'Yes.'

'Look upon the prisoner at the bar, and say whether she is guilty or not guilty.'

'*Not guilty.....*'

CHAPTER FIVE

They had brought her out by a side door.

She had been aware of faces welcoming her. . . . Roddy . . . the detective with the big moustaches. . . .

But it was to Peter Lord that she had turned.

'I want to get away. . . .'

She was with him now in the smooth Daimler, driving rapidly out of London.

He had said nothing to her. She had sat in the blessed silence.

Every minute taking her farther and farther away.

A new life. . . .

That was what she wanted. . . .

A new life.

She said suddenly:

'I—I want to go somewhere quiet . . . where there won't be any *faces*. . . .'

Peter Lord said quietly:

'That's all arranged. You're going to a sanatorium. Quiet place. Lovely gardens. No one will bother you—or get at you.'

She said with a sigh:

'Yes—that's what I want. . . .'

It was being a doctor, she supposed, that made him understand. He knew—and didn't bother her. So blessedly peaceful to be here with him, going away from it all, out of London . . . to a place that was *safe*. . . .

She wanted to forget—forget everything. . . . None of it was real any longer. It was all gone, vanished, finished with—the old life and the old emotions. She was a new, strange, defenceless creature, very crude and raw, beginning all over again. Very strange and very afraid. . . .

But it was comforting to be with Peter Lord. . . .

They were out of London now, passing through suburbs.

She said at last:

'It was all you—all you . . .'

Peter Lord said:

'It was Hercule Poirot. The fellow's a kind of magician!'

But Elinor shook her head. She said obstinately:

'It was *you*. *You* got hold of him and made him do it!'

Peter grinned.

'I made him do it all right. . . .'

Elinor said:

'Did you know I hadn't done it, or weren't you sure?'

Peter said simply:

'I was never quite sure.'

Elinor said:

'That's why I nearly said "guilty" right at the beginning . . . because, you see, I *had* thought of it. . . . I thought of it that day when I laughed outside the cottage.'

Peter said:

'Yes, I knew.'

She said wonderingly:

'It seems so queer now . . . like a kind of possession. That day I bought the paste and cut the sandwiches I was pretending to myself, I was thinking: "I've mixed poison with this, and when she eats she will die—and then Roddy will come back to me." '

Peter Lord said:

'It helps some people to pretend that sort of thing to themselves. It isn't a bad thing, really. You take it out of yourself in a fantasy. Like sweating a thing out of your system.'

Elinor said:

'Yes, that's true. Because it went—suddenly! The blackness, I mean! When that woman mentioned the rose tree outside the Lodge—it all swung back into—into being normal again. . . .'

Then with a shiver she said:

'Afterwards when we went into the morning-room and she was dead—dying, at least—I felt then: Is there much difference between *thinking* and *doing* murder?'

Peter Lord said:

'All the difference in the world!'

'Yes, but is there?'

'Of course there is! Thinking murder doesn't really do any harm. People have silly ideas about that; they think it's the same as *planning* murder! It isn't. If you think murder long enough, you suddenly come through the blackness and feel that it's all rather silly!'

Elinor cried:

'Oh! you *are* a comforting person. . . .'

Peter Lord said rather incoherently:

'Not at all. Just common sense.'

Elinor said, and there were suddenly tears in her eyes:

'Every now and then—in court—I looked at you. It gave me courage. You looked so—so *ordinary*.'

Then she laughed. 'That's rude!'

He said:

'I understand. When you're in the middle of a nightmare something ordinary is the only hope. Anyway, ordinary things are the best, I've always thought so.'

For the first time since she had entered the car she turned her head and looked at him.

The sight of his face didn't hurt her as Roddy's face always hurt her; it gave her no sharp pang of pain and pleasure mixed; instead, it made her feel warm and comforted.

She thought:

'How nice his face is . . . nice and funny—and, yes, comforting. . . .'

They drove on.

They came at last to a gateway and a drive that wound upwards till it reached a quiet white house on the side of a hill.

He said:

'You'll be quite safe here. No one will bother you.'

Impulsively she laid her hand on his arm.

She said:

'You—you'll come and see me?'
'Of course.'
'Often?'
Peter Lord said:
'As often as you want me.'
She said:
'Please come—*very often*. . . .'

CHAPTER SIX

Hercule Poirot said:

'So you see, my friend, the lies people tell are just as useful as the truth?'

Peter Lord said:

'Did everyone tell you lies?'

Hercule Poirot nodded.

'Oh, yes! For one reason or another, you comprehend. The one person to whom truth was an obligation and who was sensitive and scrupulous concerning it—that person was the one who puzzled me most!'

Peter Lord murmured:

'Elinor herself!'

'Precisely. The evidence pointed to her as the guilty party. And she herself, with her sensitive and fastidious conscience, did nothing to dispel that assumption. Accusing herself of the will, if not the deed, she came very near to abandoning a distasteful and sordid fight and pleading guilty in court to a crime she had not committed.'

Peter Lord breathed a sigh of exasperation.

'Incredible.'

Poirot shook his head.

'Not at all. She condemned herself—because she judged herself by a more exacting standard than ordinary humanity applies!'

Peter Lord said thoughtfully:

'Yes, she's like that.'

Hercule Poirot went on:

'From the moment that I started my investigations there was

always the strong possibility that Elinor Carlisle was guilty of the crime of which she was accused. But I fulfilled my obligations towards you and I discovered that a fairly strong case could be made out against another person.'

'Nurse Hopkins?'

'Not to begin with. Roderick Welman was the first person to attract my attention. In his case, again, we start with a lie. He told me that he left England on July 9th and returned on August 1st. But Nurse Hopkins had mentioned casually that Mary Gerrard had rebuffed Roderick. Welman's advances both in Maidensford "and again when she saw him in London." Mary Gerrard, you informed me, went to London on July 10th—*a day after* Roderick Welman had left England. When then did Mary Gerrard have an interview with Roderick Welman in London? I set my burglarious friend to work, and by an examination of Welman's passport I discovered that he had been in England from July 25th to the 27th. *And he had deliberately lied about it.*

'There had always been that period of time in my mind when the sandwiches were on a plate in the pantry and Elinor Carlisle was down at the Lodge. But all along I realised that in that case Elinor must have been the intended victim, not Mary. Had Roderick Welman any motive for killing Elinor Carlisle? Yes, a very good one. She had made a will leaving him her entire fortune; and by adroit questioning I discovered that Roderick Welman could have made himself acquainted with that fact.'

Peter Lord said:

'And why did you decide that he was innocent?'

'Because of one more lie. Such a silly stupid negligible little lie, too. Nurse Hopkins said that she had scratched her wrist on a rose tree, that she had got a thorn in it. And I went and saw the rose tree, and *it had no thorns.* . . . So clearly Nurse Hopkins had told a lie—and the lie was so silly and so seemingly pointless that it focused my attention upon her.

'I began to wonder about Nurse Hopkins. Up till then she had struck me as a perfectly credible witness, consistent throughout, with a strong bias against the accused arising naturally enough out of her affection for the dead girl. But now, with that silly pointless little lie in my mind, I considered Nurse Hopkins and her evidence very carefully, and I realised something that I had not been clever enough to see before.

Nurse Hopkins knew something about Mary Gerrard which she was very anxious should come out.'

Peter Lord said in surprise:

'I thought it was the other way round?'

'Ostensibly, yes. She gave a very fine performance of someone who knows something and isn't going to tell! But when I thought it over carefully I realised that every word she had said on the subject had been uttered with diametrically the opposite end in view. My conversation with Nurse O'Brien confirmed that belief. Hopkins had used her very cleverly without Nurse O'Brien being conscious of the fact.

'It was clear then that Nurse Hopkins had a game of her own to play. I contrasted the two lies, her and Roderick Welman's. Was either of them capable of an innocent explanation?

'In Roderick's case, I answered immediately: Yes. Roderick Welman is a very sensitive creature. To admit that he had been unable to keep to his plan of staying abroad, and had been compelled to slink back and hang round the girl, who would have nothing to do with him, would have been most hurtful to his pride. Since there was no question of his having been near the scene of the murder or of knowing anything about it, he took the line of least resistance and avoided unpleasantness (a most characteristic trait!) by ignoring that hurried visit to England and simply stating that he returned on August 1st when the news of the murder reached him.

'Now as to Nurse Hopkins, could there be an innocent explanation of her lie? The more I thought of it, the more extraordinary it seemed to me. *Why* should Nurse Hopkins find it necessary to lie because she had a mark on her wrist? What was the significance of that mark?

'I began to ask myself certain questions. Who did the morphine that was stolen belong to? Nurse Hopkins. Who could have administered that morphine to old Mrs. Welman? Nurse Hopkins. Yes, but why call attention to its disappearance? There could be only one answer to that if Nurse Hopkins was guilty: because the other murder, the murder of Mary Gerrard, was already planned, and a scapegoat had been selected, but that scapegoat must be shown to *have had a chance of obtaining morphine.*

'Certain other things fitted in. The anonymous letter written to Elinor. That was to create bad feeling between Elinor and

Mary. The idea doubtless was that Elinor would come down and object to Mary's influence over Mrs. Welman. The fact that Roderick Welman fell violently in love with Mary was, of course, a totally unforeseen circumstance—but one that Nurse Hopkins was quick to appreciate. Here was a perfect motive for the scapegoat. Elinor.

'But what was the *reason* for the two crimes? What motive could there be for Nurse Hopkins to do away with Mary Gerrard? I began to see a light—oh, very dim as yet. Nurse Hopkins had a good deal of influence over Mary, and one of the ways she had used that influence was to induce the girl *to make a will*. But the will did not benefit Nurse Hopkins. It benefited an aunt of Mary's who lived in New Zealand. And then I remembered a chance remark that someone in the village had made to me. That aunt had been a hospital nurse.

'The light was not quite so dim now. The pattern—the design of the crime—was becoming apparent. The next step was easy. I visited Nurse Hopkins once more. We both played the comedy very prettily. In the end she allowed herself to be persuaded to tell what she had been aiming to tell all along! Only she tells it, perhaps, just a little sooner than she meant to do! But the opportunity is so good that she cannot resist. And, after all, the truth has got to be known some time. So, with well-feigned reluctance, she produces the letter. And then, my friend, it is no longer conjecture. I *know*! The letter gives her away.'

Peter Lord frowned and said:

'How?'

'*Mon cher!* The superscription on that letter was as follows: "For Mary, to be sent to her after my death." But the gist of the contents made it perfectly plain that Mary *Gerrard* was not to know the truth. Also, the word *sent* (not *given*) on the envelope was illuminating. It was not Mary *Gerrard* to whom that letter was written, but another Mary. It was to her sister, Mary *Riley*, in New Zealand, that Eliza Riley wrote the truth.

'Nurse Hopkins did not find that letter at the Lodge after Mary Gerrard's death. She had had it in her possession for many years. She received it in New Zealand, where it was sent to her after her sister's death.'

He paused.

'Once one had seen the truth with the eyes of the mind the rest was easy. The quickness of air travel made it possible for a witness who knew Mary Draper well in New Zealand to be present in court.'

Peter Lord said:

'Supposing you had been wrong and Nurse Hopkins and Mary Draper had been two entirely different people?'

Poirot said coldly:

'I am never wrong!'

Peter Lord laughed.

Hercule Poirot went on:

'My friend, we know something now of this woman Mary Riley or Draper. The police of New Zealand were unable to get sufficient evidence for a conviction, but they had been watching her for some time when she suddenly left the country. There was a patient of hers, an old lady, who left her "dear Nurse Riley" a very snug little legacy, and whose death was somewhat of a puzzle to the doctor attending her. Mary Draper's husband insured his life in her favour for a considerable sum, and his death was sudden and unaccountable. Unfortunately for her, though he had made out a cheque to the Insurance Company, he had forgotten to post it. Other deaths may lie at her door. It is certain she is a remorseless and unscrupulous woman.

'One can imagine that her sister's letter suggested possibilities to her resourceful mind. When New Zealand became too hot, as you say, to hold her, and she came to this country and resumed her profession in the name of Hopkins (a former colleague of hers in hospital who died abroad), Maidensford was her objective. She may perhaps have contemplated some form of blackmail. But old Mrs. Welman was not the kind of woman to allow herself to be blackmailed, and Nurse Riley, or Hopkins, very wisely did not attempt anything of the sort. Doubtless she made inquiries and discovered that Mrs. Welman was a very wealthy woman, and some chance word of Mrs. Welman's may have revealed the fact that the old lady had not made a will.

'So, on that June evening, when Nurse O'Brien retailed to her colleague that Mrs. Welman was asking for her lawyer, Hopkins did not hesitate. Mrs. Welman must die intestate so that her illegitimate daughter would inherit her money. Hopkins had already made friends with Mary Gerrard and acquired a good deal of influence over the girl. All that she had to do now was to persuade the girl to make a will leaving her money to her mother's sister; and she inspired the word-

186

ing of that will very carefully. There was no mention of the relationship: just "Mary Riley, sister of the late Eliza Riley." Once that was signed, Mary Gerrard was doomed. The woman only had to wait for a suitable opportunity. She had, I fancy, already planned the method of the crime, with the use of the apomorphine to secure her own alibi. She may have meant to get Elinor and Mary to her cottage, but when Elinor came down to the Lodge and asked them both to come up and have sandwiches she realised at once that a perfect opportunity had arisen. The circumstances were such that Elinor was practically certain to be convicted.'

Peter Lord said slowly:

'If it hadn't been for you—she would have been convicted.'

Hercule Poirot said quickly:

'No, it is you, my friend, she has to thank for her life.'

'I? I didn't do anything. I tried——'

He broke off, Hercule Poirot smiled a little.

'*Mais oui*, you tried very hard, did you not? You were impatient because I did not seem to you to be getting anywhere. And you were afraid, too, that she might, after all, be guilty. And so, with great impertinence, you also told me the lies! But, *mon cher*, you were not very clever about it. In future I advise you to stick to the measles and the whooping-cough and leave crime detection alone.'

Peter Lord blushed.

He said:

'Did you know—all the time?'

Poirot said severely:

'You lead me by the hand to a clearing in the shrubs, and you assist me to find a German matchbox that you have just put there! *C'est l'enfantillage!*'

Peter Lord winced.

He groaned:

'Rub it in!'

Poirot went on:

'You converse with the gardener and lead him to say that he saw your car in the road; and then you give a start and pretend that it was *not* your car. And you look hard at me to make sure that I realise that someone, a stranger, must have been there that morning.'

'I was a damned fool,' said Peter Lord.

'What were you doing at Hunterbury that morning?'

Peter Lord blushed.

'It was just sheer idiocy. . . . I—I'd heard she was down. I went up to the house on the chance of seeing her. I didn't mean to speak to her. I—I just wanted to—well—see her. From the path in the shrubbery I saw her in the pantry cutting bread and butter——'

'Charlotte and the poet Werther. Continue, my friend.'

'Oh, there's nothing to tell. I just slipped into the bushes and stayed there watching her till she went away.'

Poirot said gently:

'Did you fall in love with Elinor Carlisle the first time you saw her?'

There was a long silence.

'I suppose so.'

Then Peter Lord said:

'Oh, well, I suppose she and Roderick Welman will live happy ever afterwards.'

Hercule Poirot said:

'My dear friend, you suppose nothing of the sort!'

'Why not? She'll forgive him the Mary Gerrard business. It was only a wild infatuation on his part, anyway.'

Hercule Poirot said:

'It goes deeper than that. . . . There is, sometimes, a deep chasm between the past and the future. When one has walked in the valley of the shadow of death, and come out of it into the sunshine—then, *mon cher*, it is a new life that begins. . . . The past will not serve. . . .'

He waited a minute and then went on:

'A new life. . . . That is what Elinor Carlisle is beginning now—and it is you who have given her that life.'

'No.'

'Yes. It was your determination, your arrogant insistence, that compelled me to do as you asked. Admit now, it is to you she turns in gratitude, is it not?'

Peter Lord said slowly:

'Yes, she's very grateful—now. . . . She asked me to go and see her—often.'

'Yes, she needs you.'

Peter Lord said violently:

'Not as she needs—him!'

Hercule Poirot shook his head.

'She never *needed* Roderick Welman. She loved him, yes, un-happily—even desperately.'

Peter Lord, his face set and grim, said harshly:

'She will never love me like that.'

Hercule Poirot said softly:

'Perhaps not. But she needs you, my friend, because it is only with you that she can begin the world again.'

Peter Lord said nothing.

Hercule Poirot's voice was very gentle as he said:

'Can you not accept *facts*? She loved Roderick Welman. What of it? With you, *she can be happy....*'

Agatha Christie

The most popular and prolific writer of detective fiction ever known, her intricately plotted whodunits are enjoyed by armchair crime-solvers all over the world. How many of these have you read?

Hallowe'en Party 30p

By the Pricking of My Thumbs 30p

Endless Night 30p

Third Girl 25p

Murder at the Vicarage 25p

One, Two, Buckle My Shoe 25p

Lord Edgware Dies 30p

After the Funeral 25p

The Mystery of the Blue Train 25p

The Pale Horse 25p

Death in the Clouds 25p

Three Act Tragedy 25p

Death on the Nile 30p

The Hollow 30p

The Sittaford Mystery 25p

Taken at the Flood 25p

At Bertram's Hotel 25p

4.50 From Paddington 25p

A Caribbean Mystery 25p

The ABC Murders 25p

The Big Four 25p

Hickory Dickory Dock 25p

The Hound of Death 25p

The Mirror Crack'd from Side to Side 25p

Murder in the Mews 25p

Partners in Crime 25p

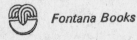 *Fontana Books*

Ngaio Marsh

'The finest writer in the English language of the pure, classical, puzzle whodunit. Among the Crime Queens, Ngaio Marsh stands out as an Empress.' *Sun.* 'Her work is as near flawless as makes no odds: character, plot, wit, good writing and sound technique.' *Sunday Times.* 'The brilliant Ngaio Marsh ranks with Agatha Christie and Dorothy Sayers.' *Times Literary Supplement*

When in Rome *30p*
Clutch of Constables *30p*
Death at the Bar *30p*
Final Curtain *30p*
Scales of Justice *30p*
Surfeit of Lampreys *30p*
Colour Scheme *30p*
Off With His Head *30p*
Vintage Murder *30p*
False Scent *30p*
Died in the Wool *30p*
Spinsters in Jeopardy *30p*
Death at the Dolphin *30p*
A Man Lay Dead *30p*
Death in a White Tie *30p*
Hand in Glove *30p*
Death in Ecstasy *30p*
Singing in the Shrouds *30p*
Artists in Crime *30p*
Enter a Murderer *30p*

 *Fontana Books*

Fontana Books

Fontana is best known as one of the leading paperback publishers of popular fiction and non-fiction. It also includes an outstanding, and expanding section of books on history, natural history, religion and social sciences.

Most of the fiction authors need no introduction. They include Agatha Christie, Hammond Innes, Alistair MacLean, Catherine Gaskin, Victoria Holt and Lucy Walker. Desmond Bagley and Maureen Peters are among the relative newcomers.

The non-fiction list features a superb collection of animal books by such favourites as Gerald Durrell and Joy Adamson.

All Fontana books are available at your bookshop or newsagent; or can be ordered direct. Just fill in the form below and list the titles you want.

7. 12. 42

FONTANA BOOKS, Cash Sales Department, P.O. Box 4, Godalming, Surrey. Please send purchase price plus 5p postage per book by cheque, postal or money order. No currency.

NAME (Block letters)

ADDRESS